H.G. WELLS'S

THE TIME MACHINE

A GRAPHIC NOVEL

BY TERRY DAVIS &
JOSÉ ALFONSO OCAMPO RUIZ

STONE ARCH BOOKS
A CAPSTONE IMPRINT

Graphic Revolve is published by Stone Arch Books
A Capstone Imprint
1710 Roe Crest Drive, North Mankato, Minnesota 56003
www.capstonepub.com

Cataloging-in-Publication Data is available at the Library
of Congress website.
Hardcover ISBN: 978-1-4965-0011-3
Paperback ISBN: 978-1-4965-0030-4

Summary: A scientist invents a machine that carries him
into the future. While there, he meets a race of gentle
humans — and evil underground creatures. Even worse,
his time machine, his only chance to escape, is trapped
deep inside the Morlock caverns.

Common Core back matter written by Dr. Katie Monnin.

Designer: Bob Lentz
Assistant Designer: Peggie Carley
Editor: Donald Lemke
Assistant Editor: Sean Tulien
Creative Director: Heather Kindseth
Editorial Director: Michael Dahl
Publisher: Ashley C. Andersen Zantop

Printed in the United States   4995

TABLE OF CONTENTS

ABOUT THE FUTURE

In *The Time Machine*, H.G. Wells imagined a very different world 800 centuries from now. But what do scientists think the future will really be like compared to Wells's predictions?

Scientists believe the Sun has already used up half of its energy. Luckily, this enormous ball of gas should keep burning for another 5 billion years. In the story, the Time Traveler thinks the Sun seems closer and bigger. Scientists believe this could actually come true. As the Sun burns out, it will also grow and expand. Eventually, it could reach the Earth — and absorb it.

Scientists indicate that before the Sun dies, the Earth will get hotter. They call the increasing temperatures global warming. Many believe that pollution could be clogging the air and trapping heat in our atmosphere. Even by the year 2100, they think the Earth could be several degrees warmer on average.

Will Morlocks and Eloi roam the earth in the future? Probably not, but there will be plenty of people! Today, the planet's total population is over 6 billion. By the year 2050, scientists estimate the population will be more than 9 billion.

Before any of these events happen, though, some scientists think humans will be living on other planets. In fact, the Mars One project hopes to have a settlement on the planet Mars by the year 2024, and they are currently accepting applications for this long, one-way trip!

CAST OF CHARACTERS

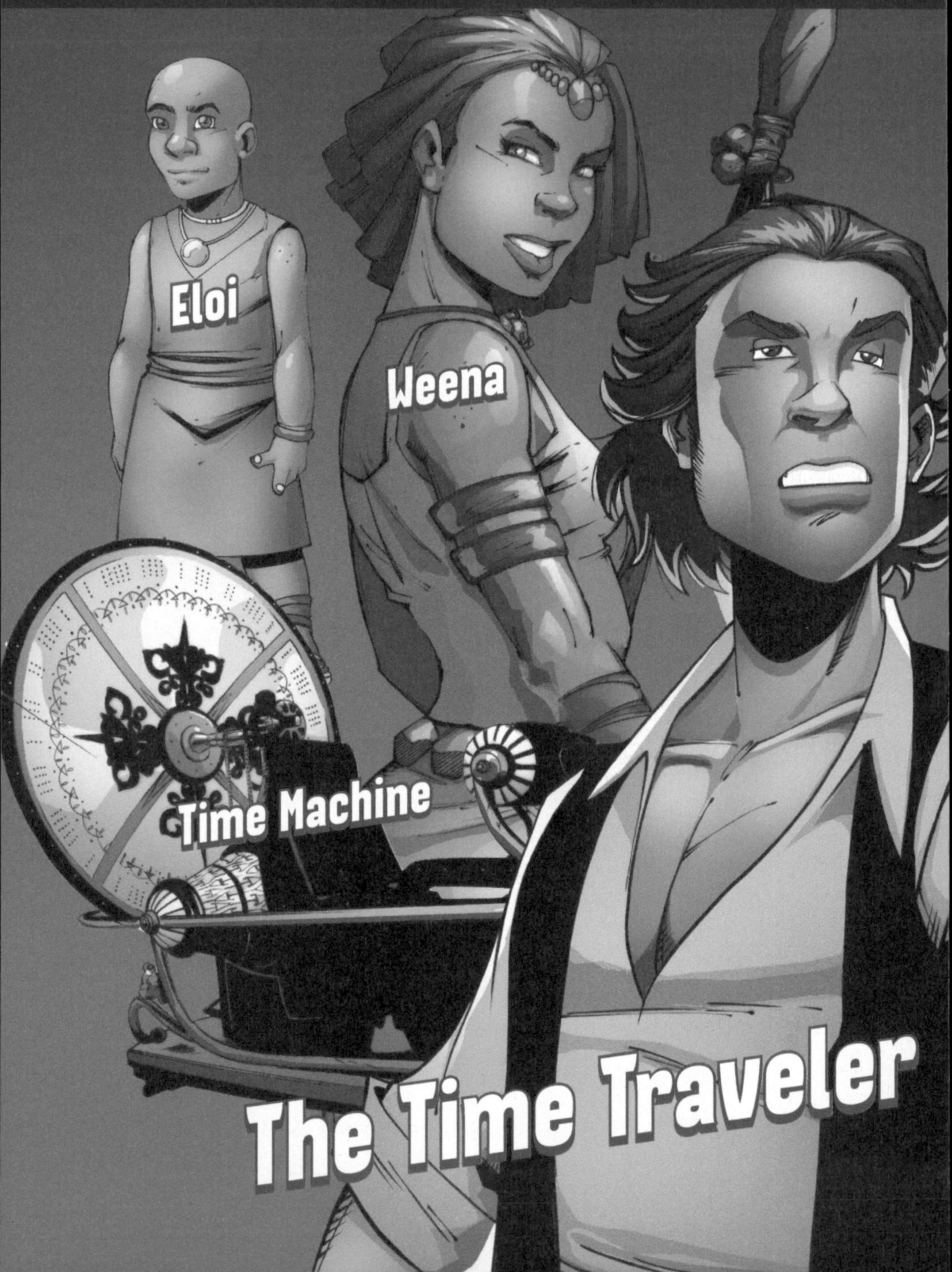
Eloi
Weena
Time Machine
The Time Traveler

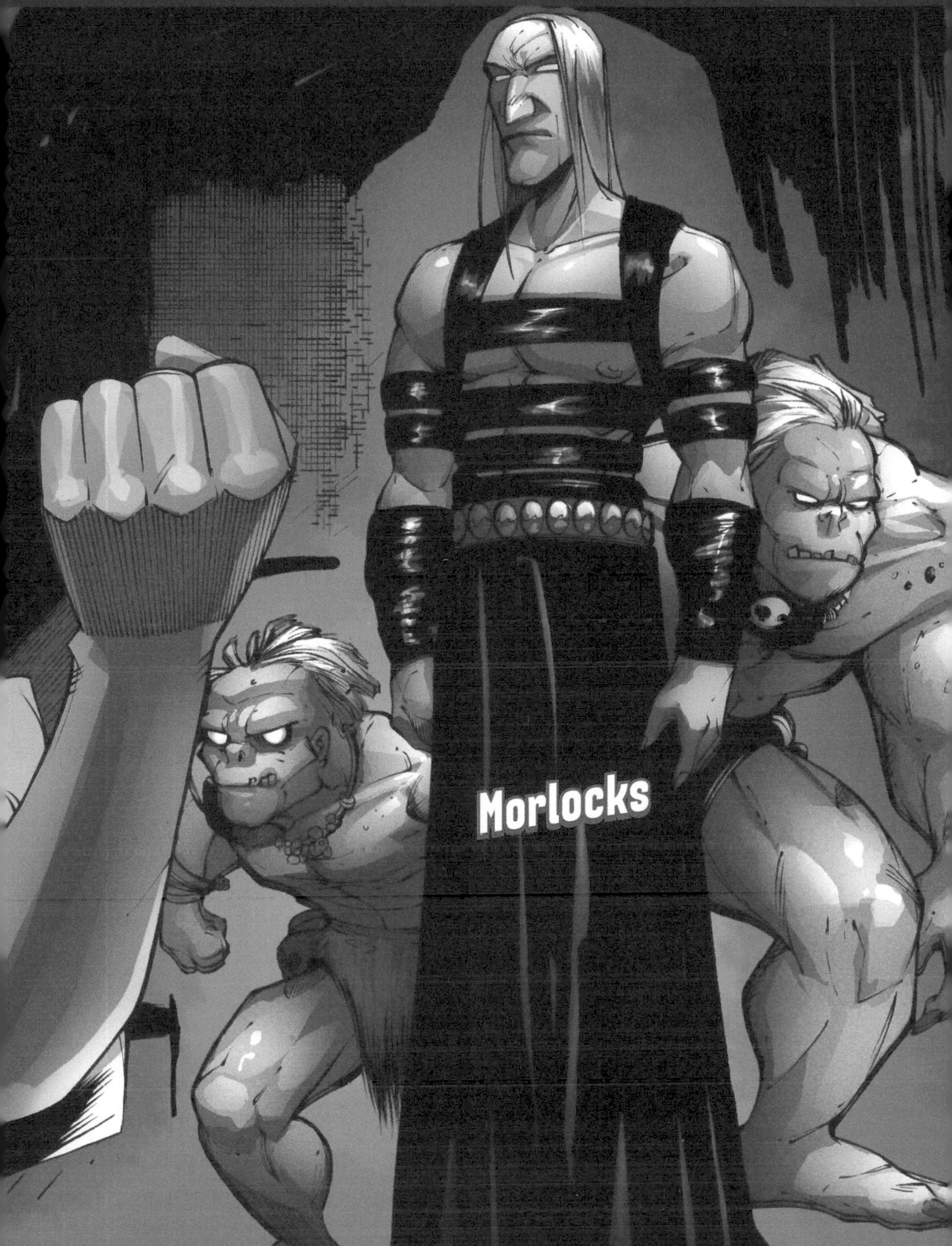
Morlocks

CHAPTER 1

NO ONE BELIEVES HIM

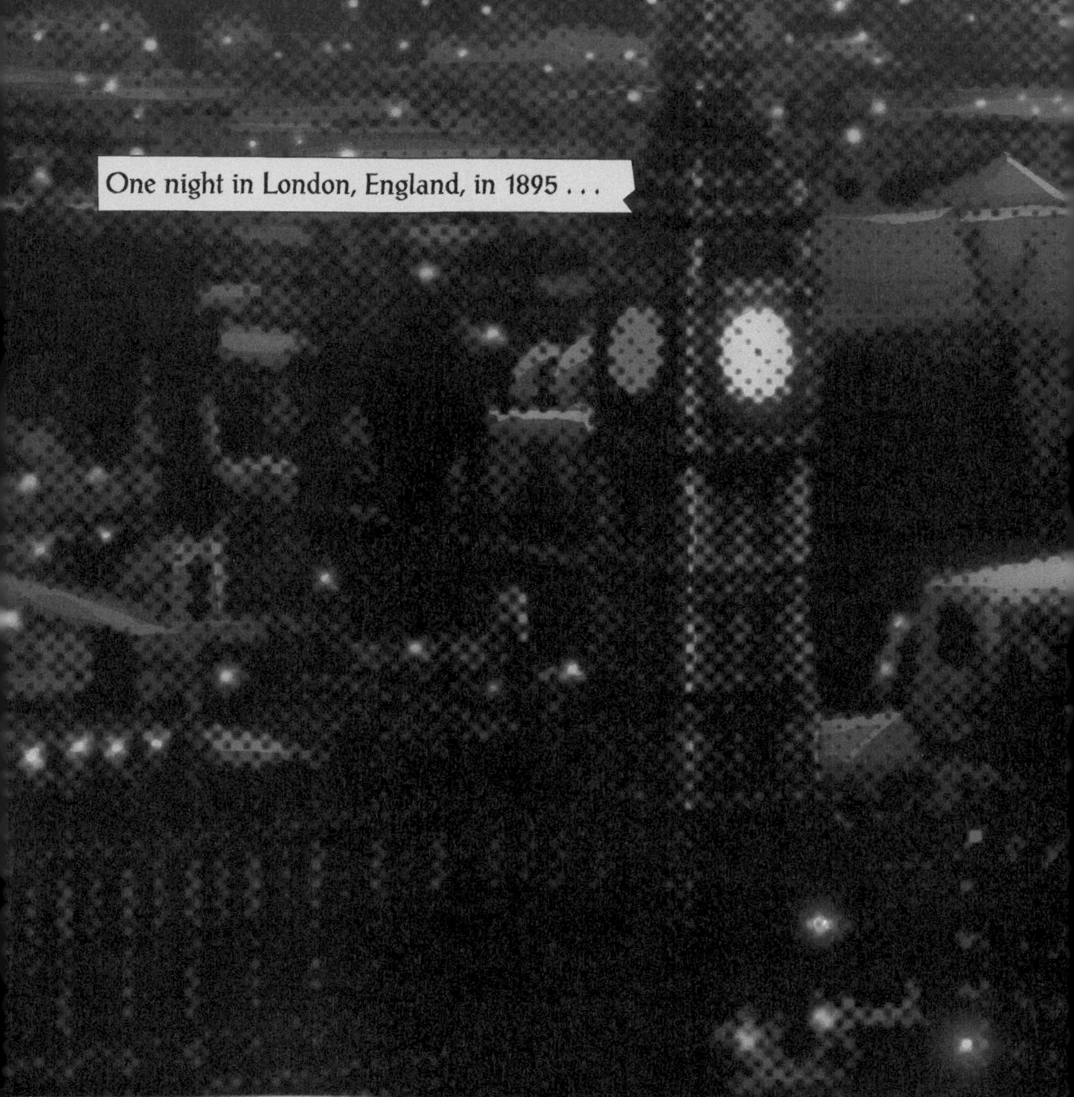
One night in London, England, in 1895 . . .

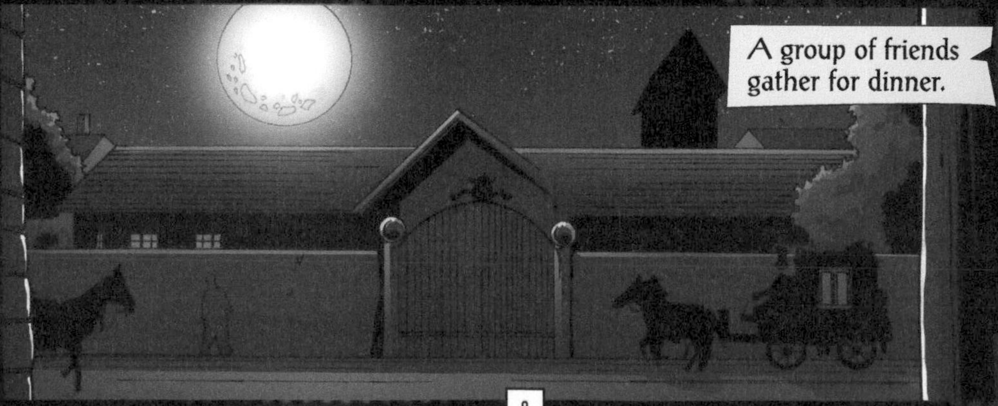
A group of friends gather for dinner.

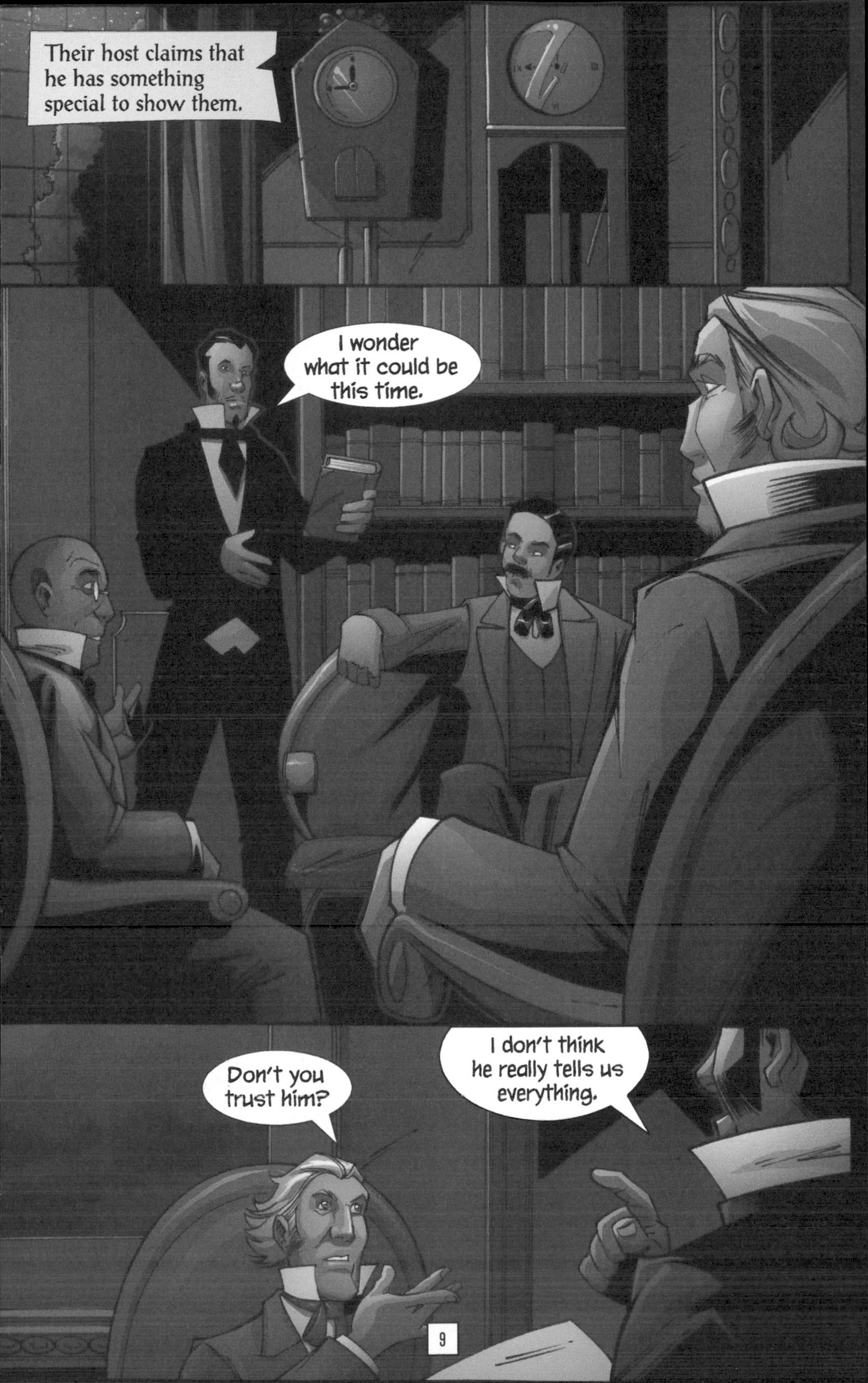

Their host claims that he has something special to show them.
I wonder what it could be this time.
Don't you trust him?
I don't think he really tells us everything.

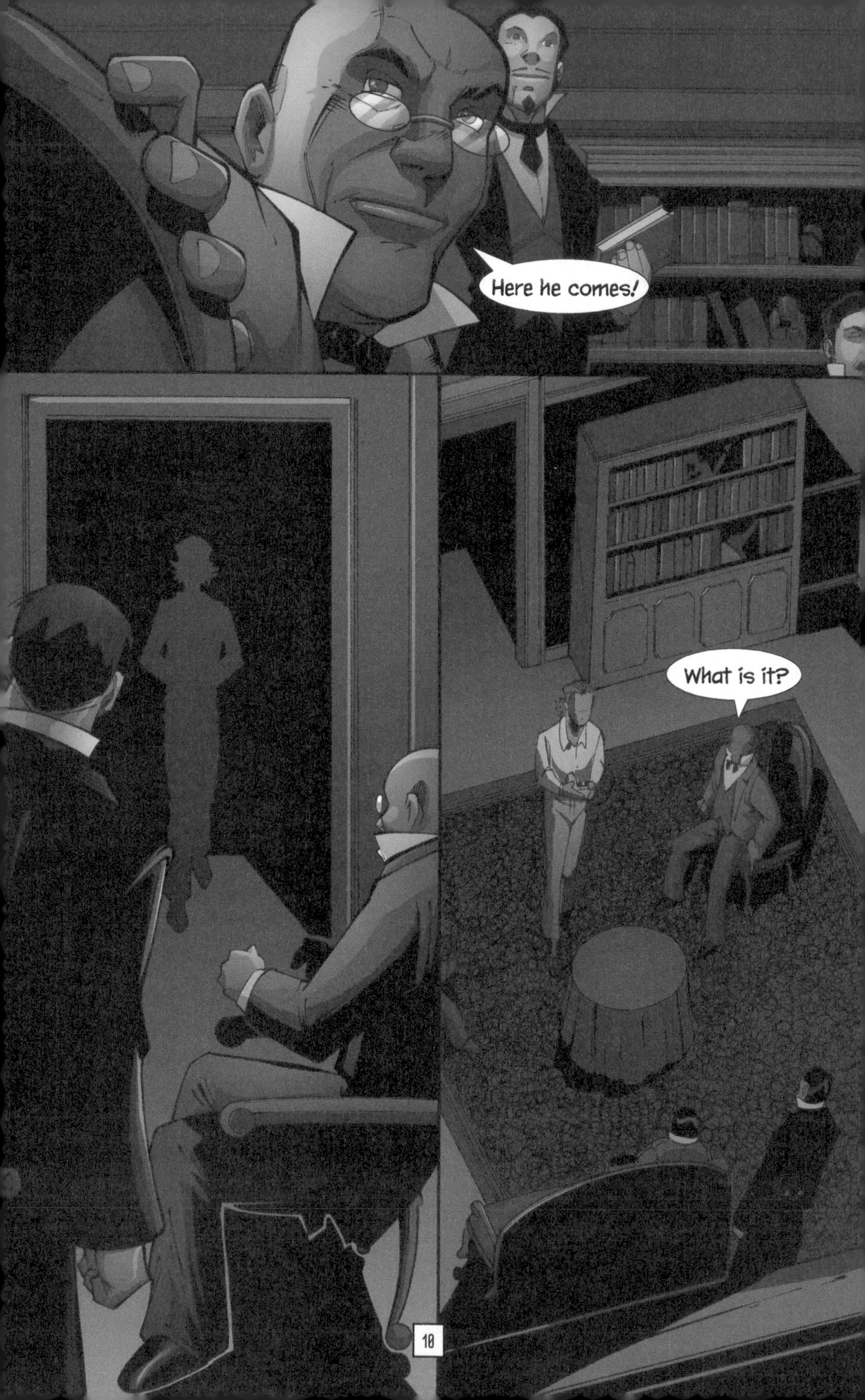
Here he comes!
What is it?

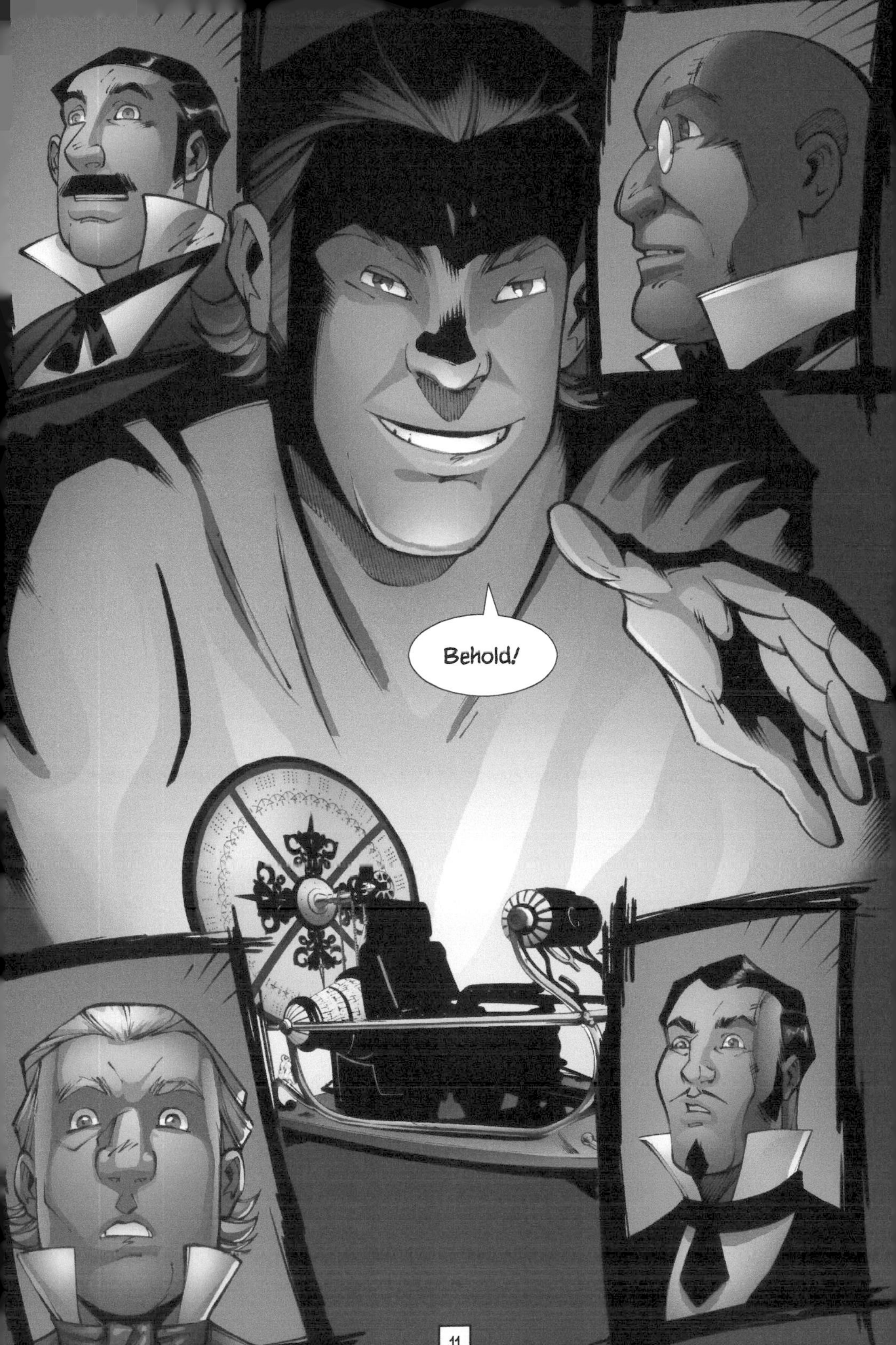
Behold!

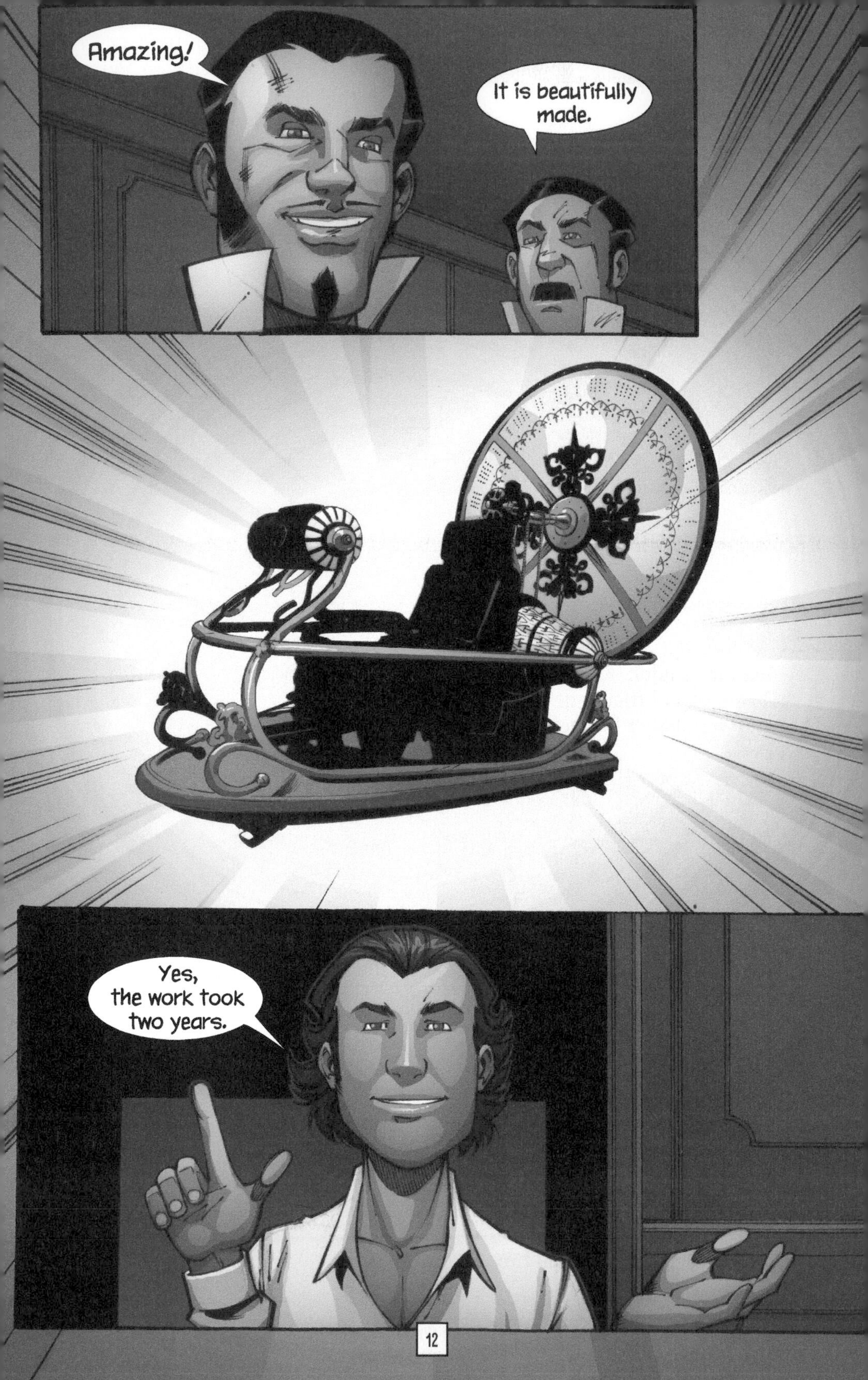
Amazing!
It is beautifully made.
Yes, the work took two years.

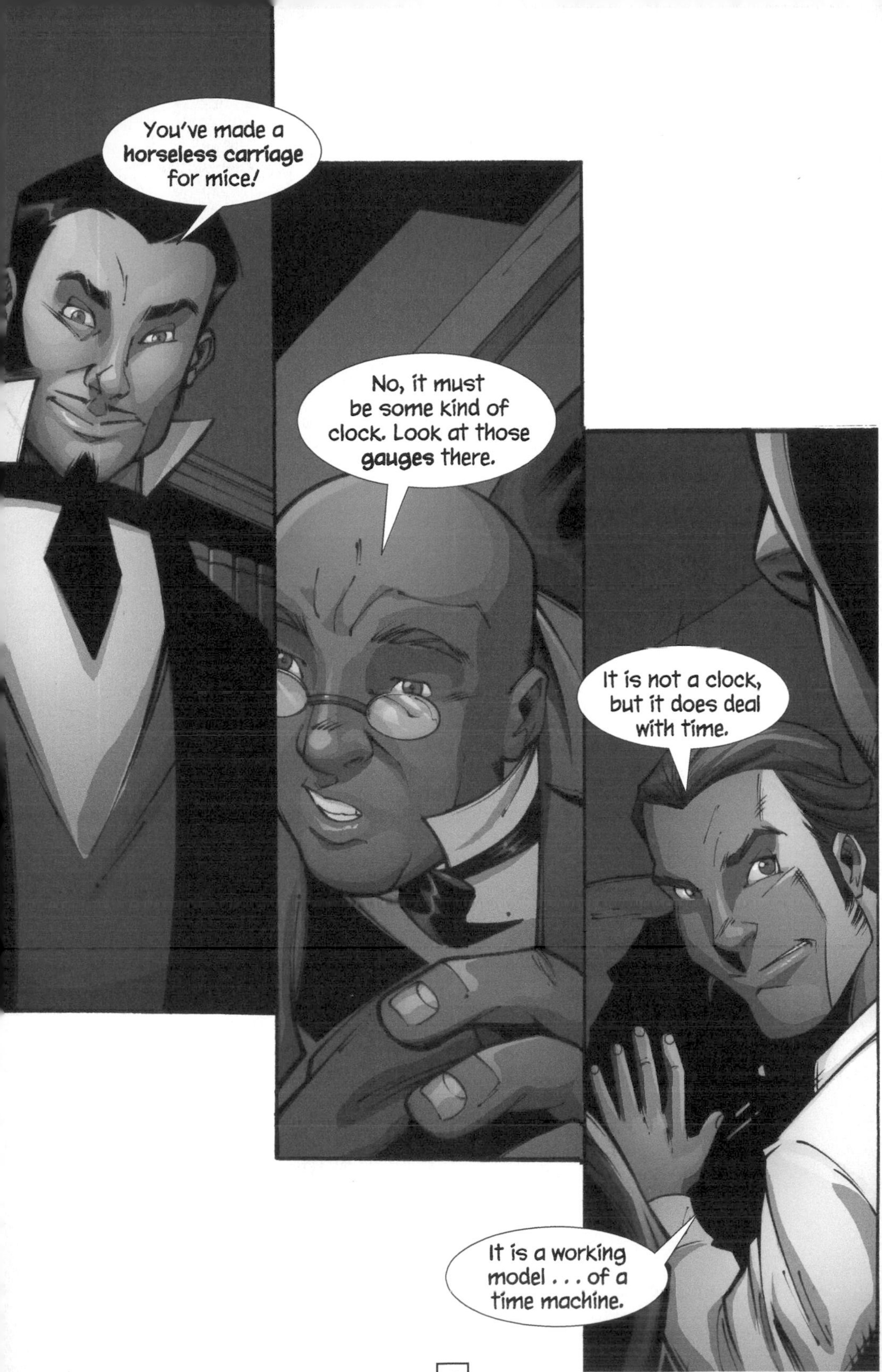
You've made a horseless carriage for mice!
No, it must be some kind of clock. Look at those gauges there.
It is not a clock, but it does deal with time.
It is a working model . . . of a time machine.

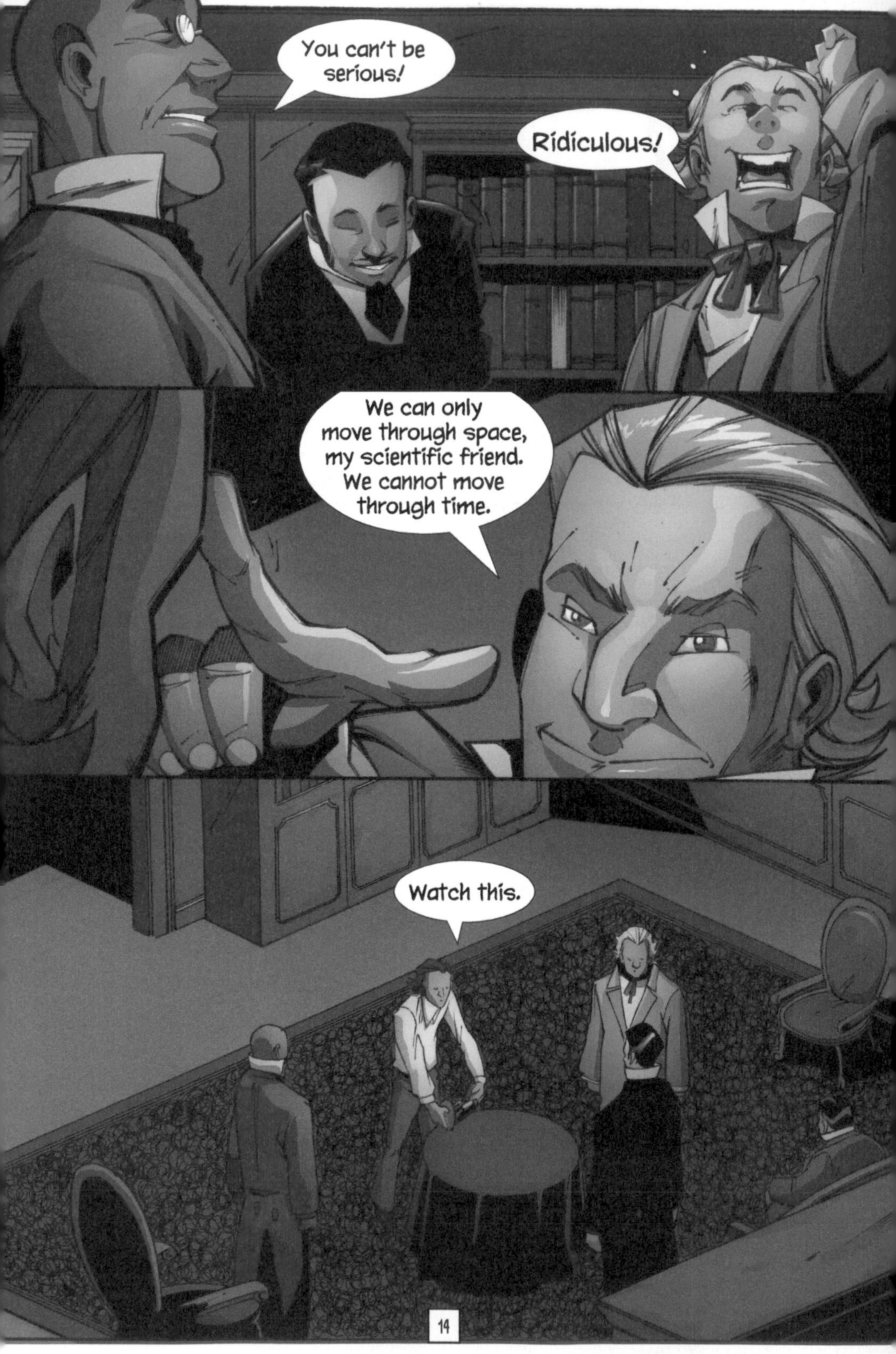
You can't be serious!
Ridiculous!
We can only move through space, my scientific friend. We cannot move through time.
Watch this.

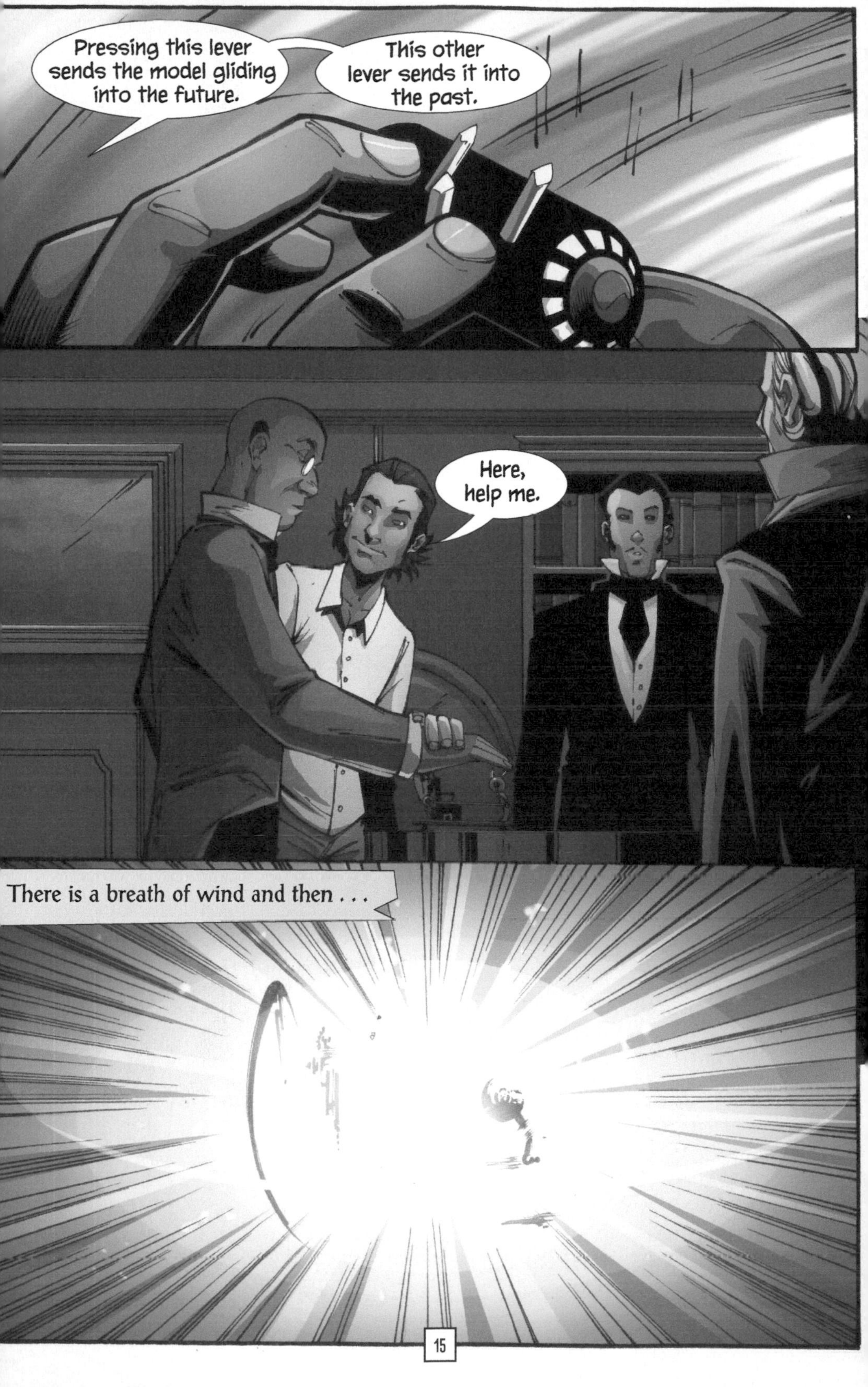

Pressing this lever sends the model gliding into the future.
This other lever sends it into the past.
Here, help me.
There is a breath of wind and then . . .

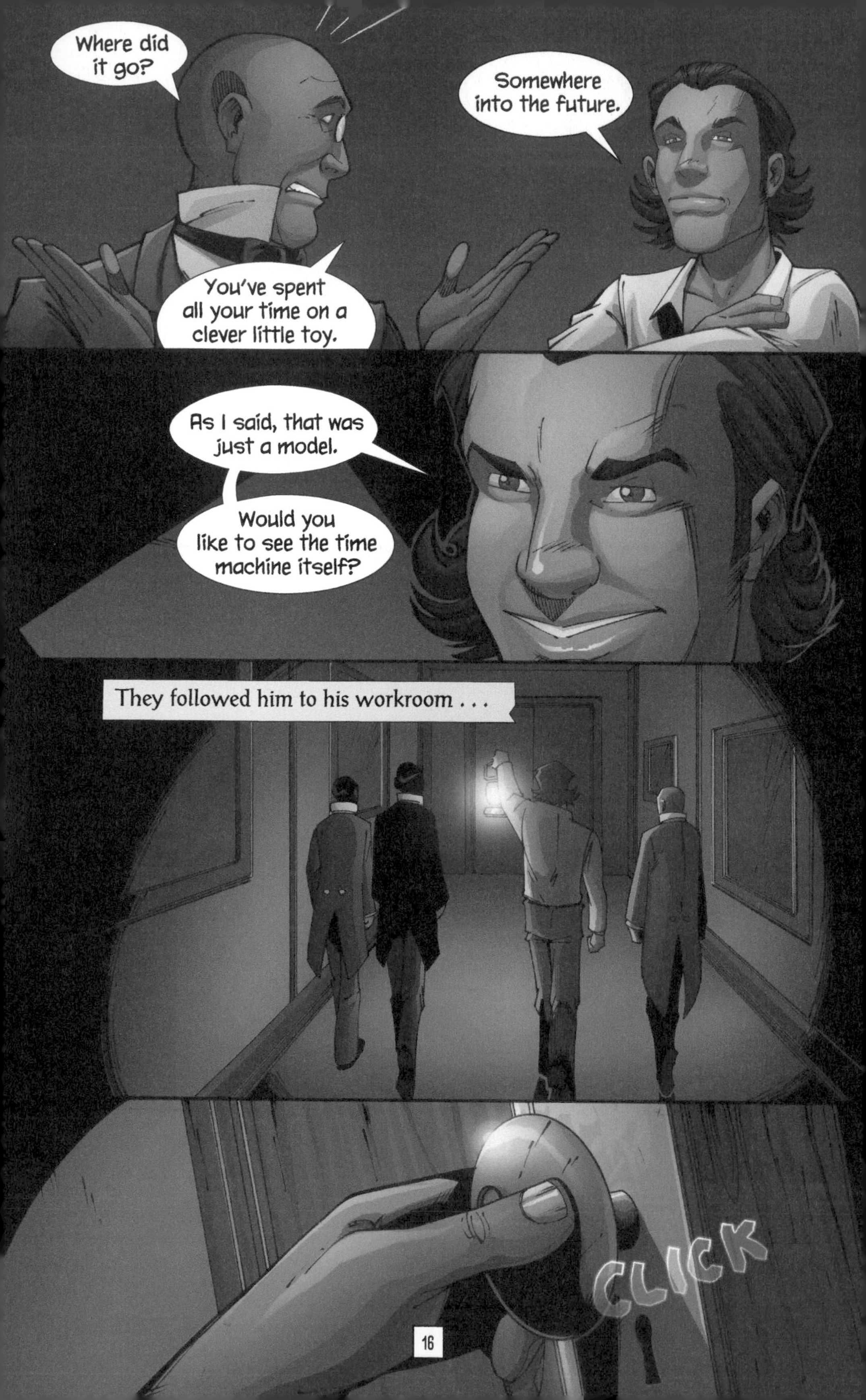
Where did it go?
Somewhere into the future.
You've spent all your time on a clever little toy.
As I said, that was just a model.
Would you like to see the time machine itself?
They followed him to his workroom . . .
CLICK

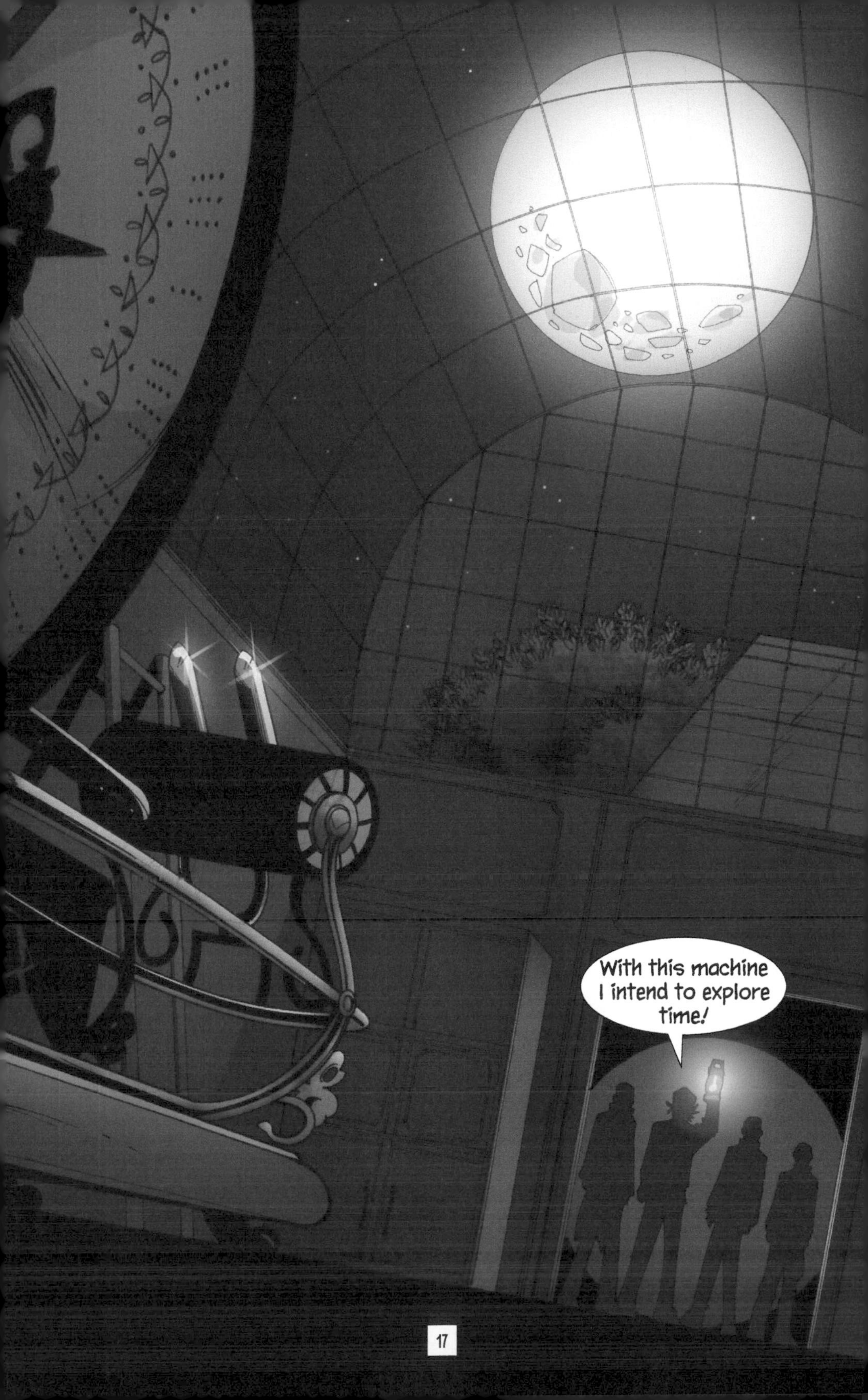
With this machine I intend to explore time!

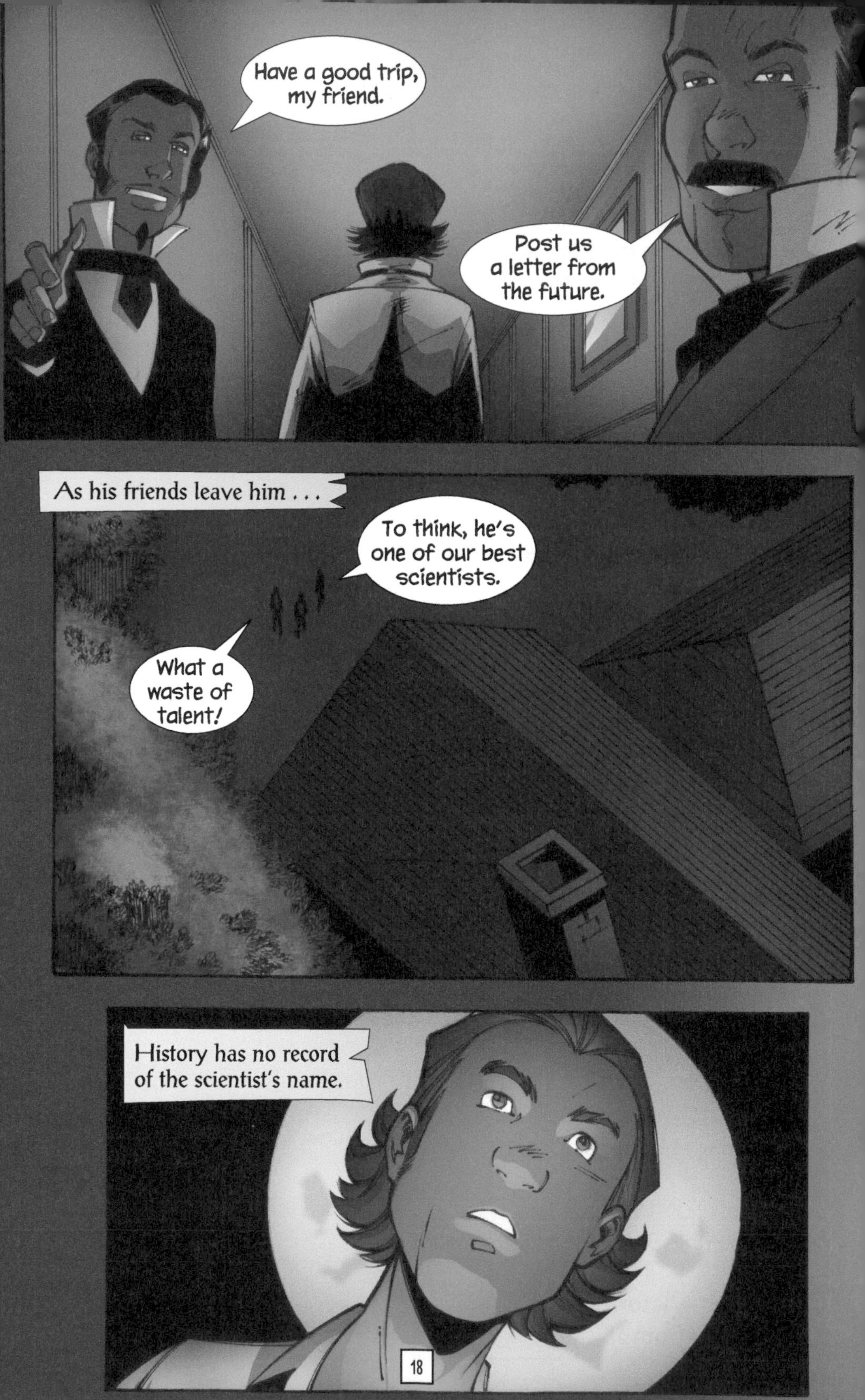
Have a good trip, my friend.
Post us a letter from the future.
As his friends leave him . . .
To think, he's one of our best scientists.
What a waste of talent!
History has no record of the scientist's name.

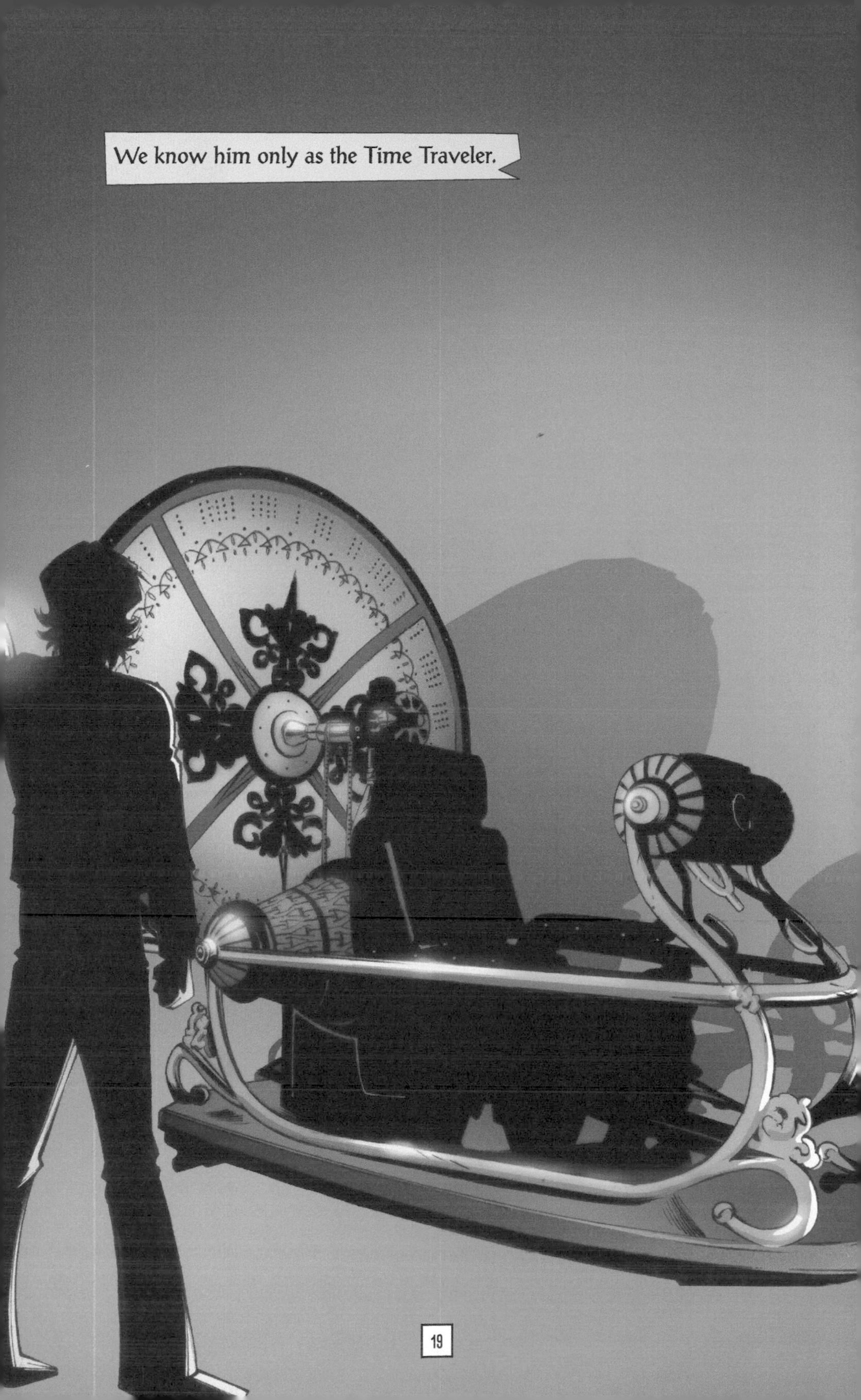
We know him only as the Time Traveler.

CHAPTER 2
INTO THE FUTURE

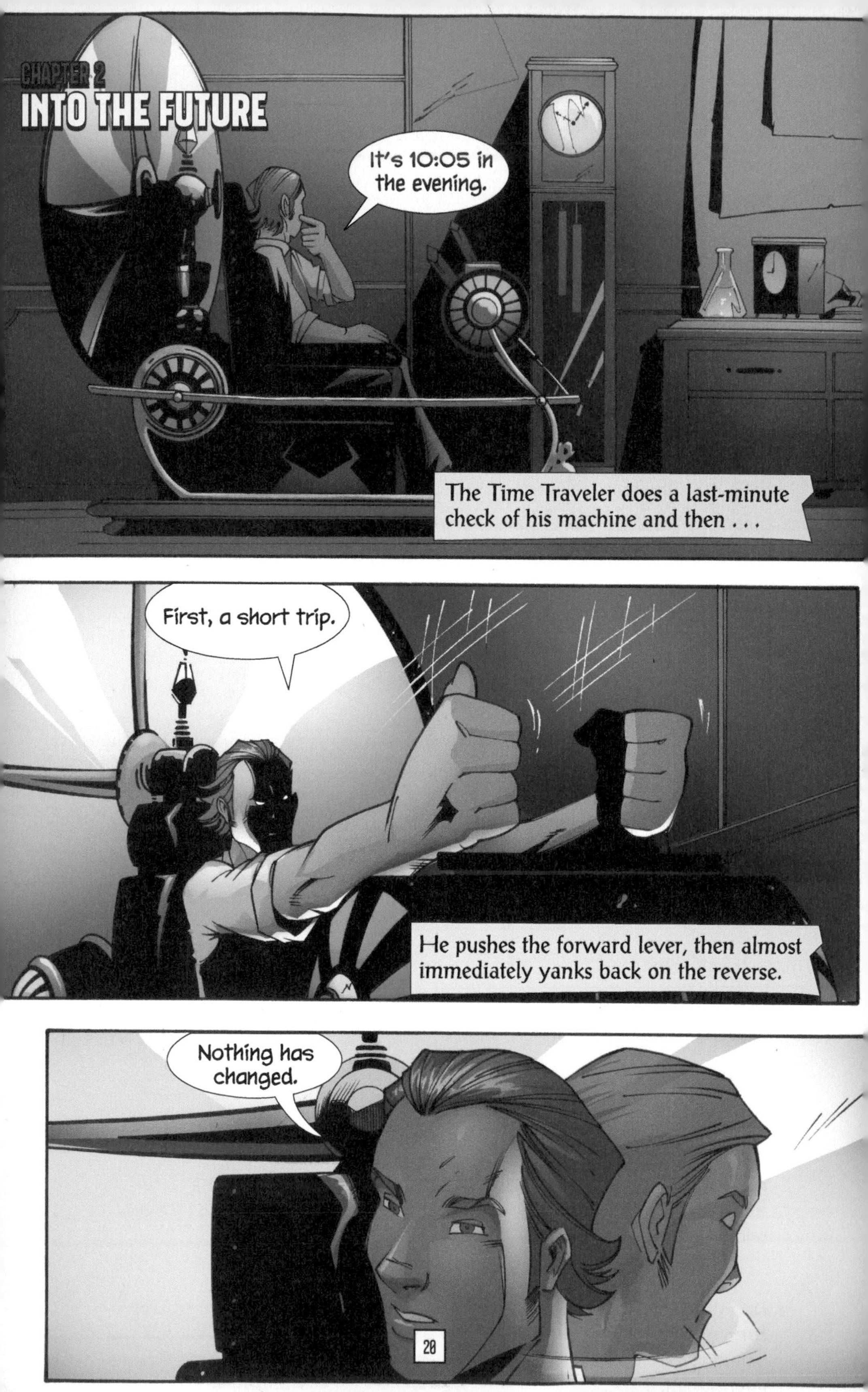
It's 10:05 in the evening.
The Time Traveler does a last-minute check of his machine and then . . .
First, a short trip.
He pushes the forward lever, then almost immediately yanks back on the reverse.
Nothing has changed.

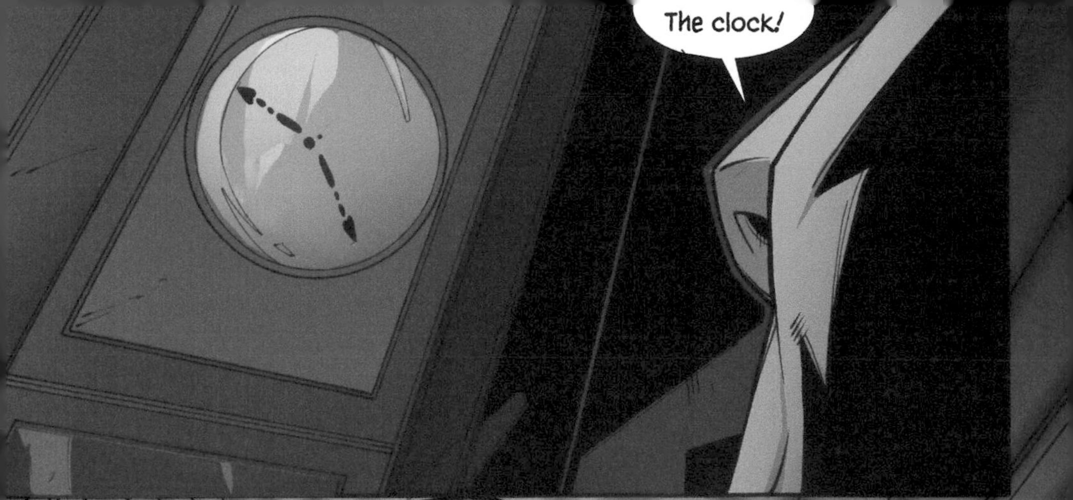
The clock!

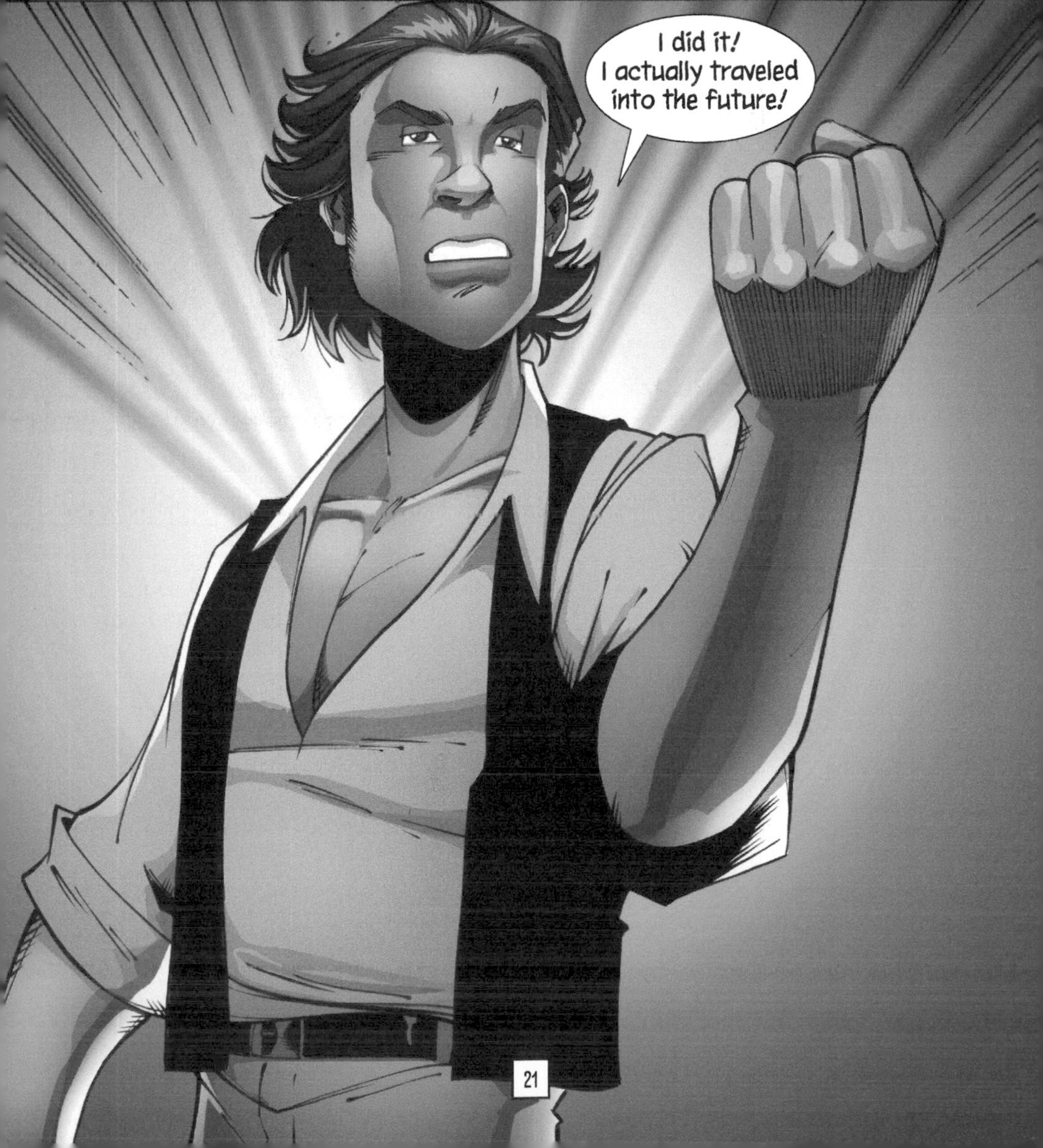
I did it!
I actually traveled into the future!

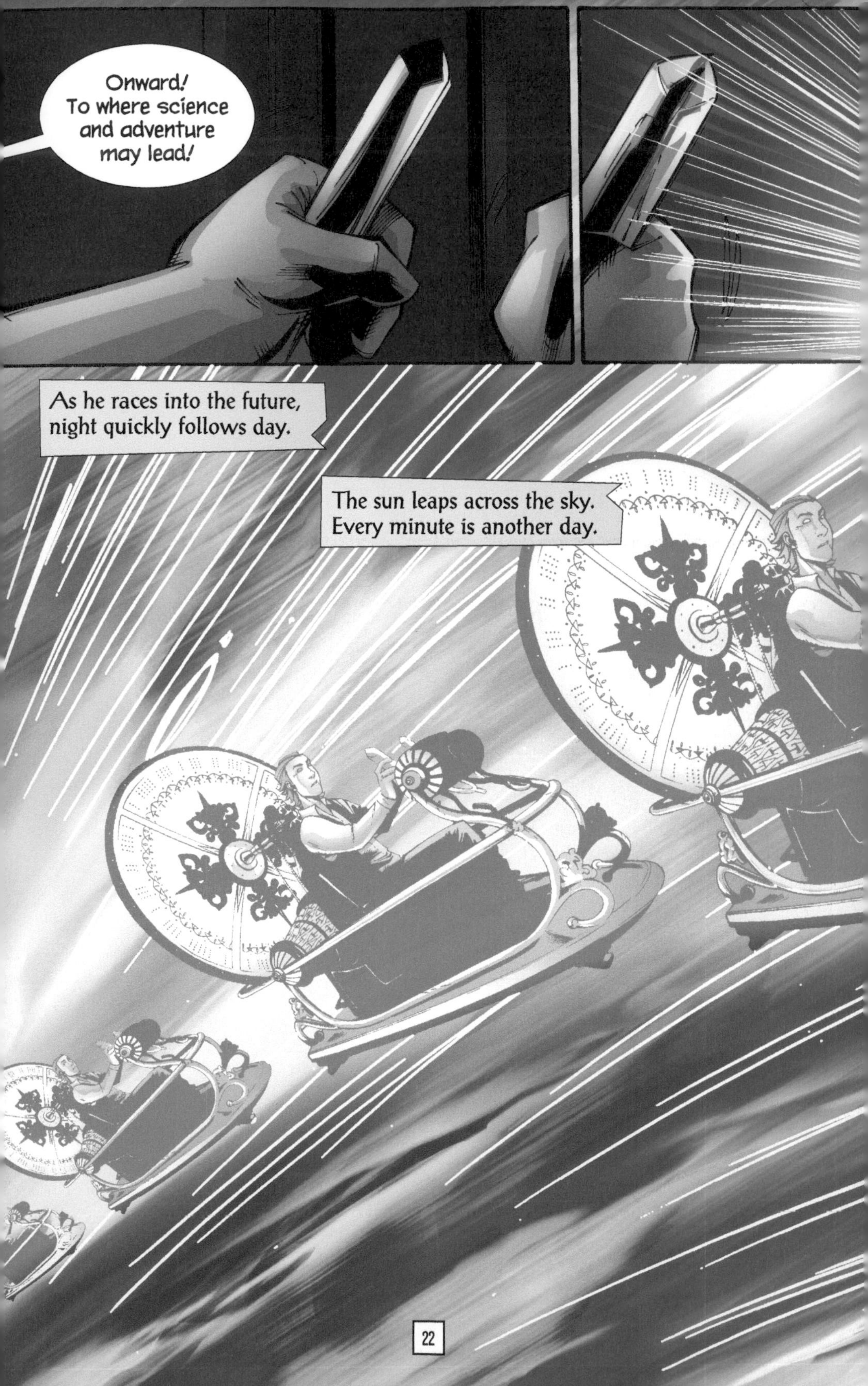
Onward! To where science and adventure may lead!
As he races into the future, night quickly follows day.
The sun leaps across the sky. Every minute is another day.

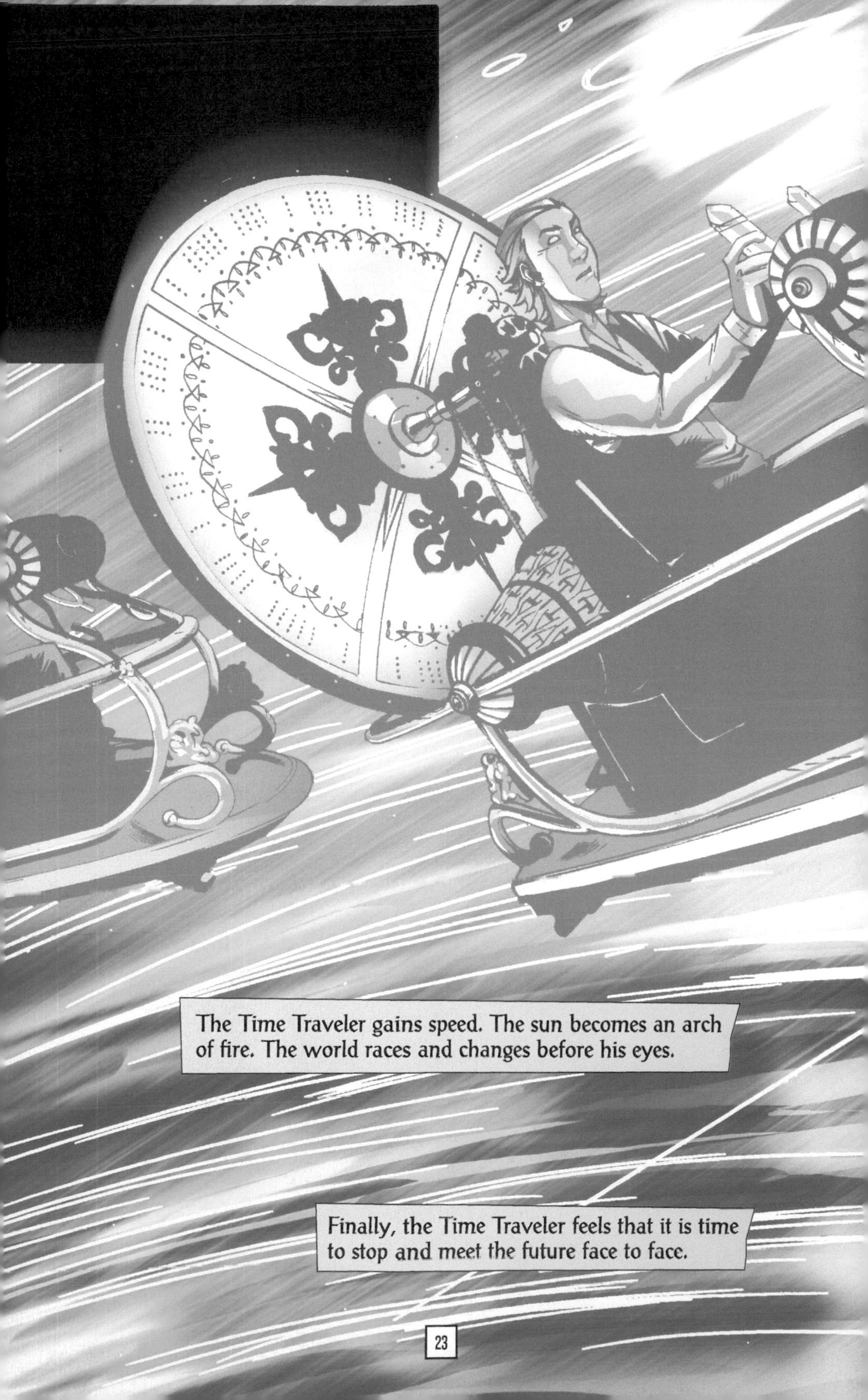
The Time Traveler gains speed. The sun becomes an arch of fire. The world races and changes before his eyes.
Finally, the Time Traveler feels that it is time to stop and meet the future face to face.

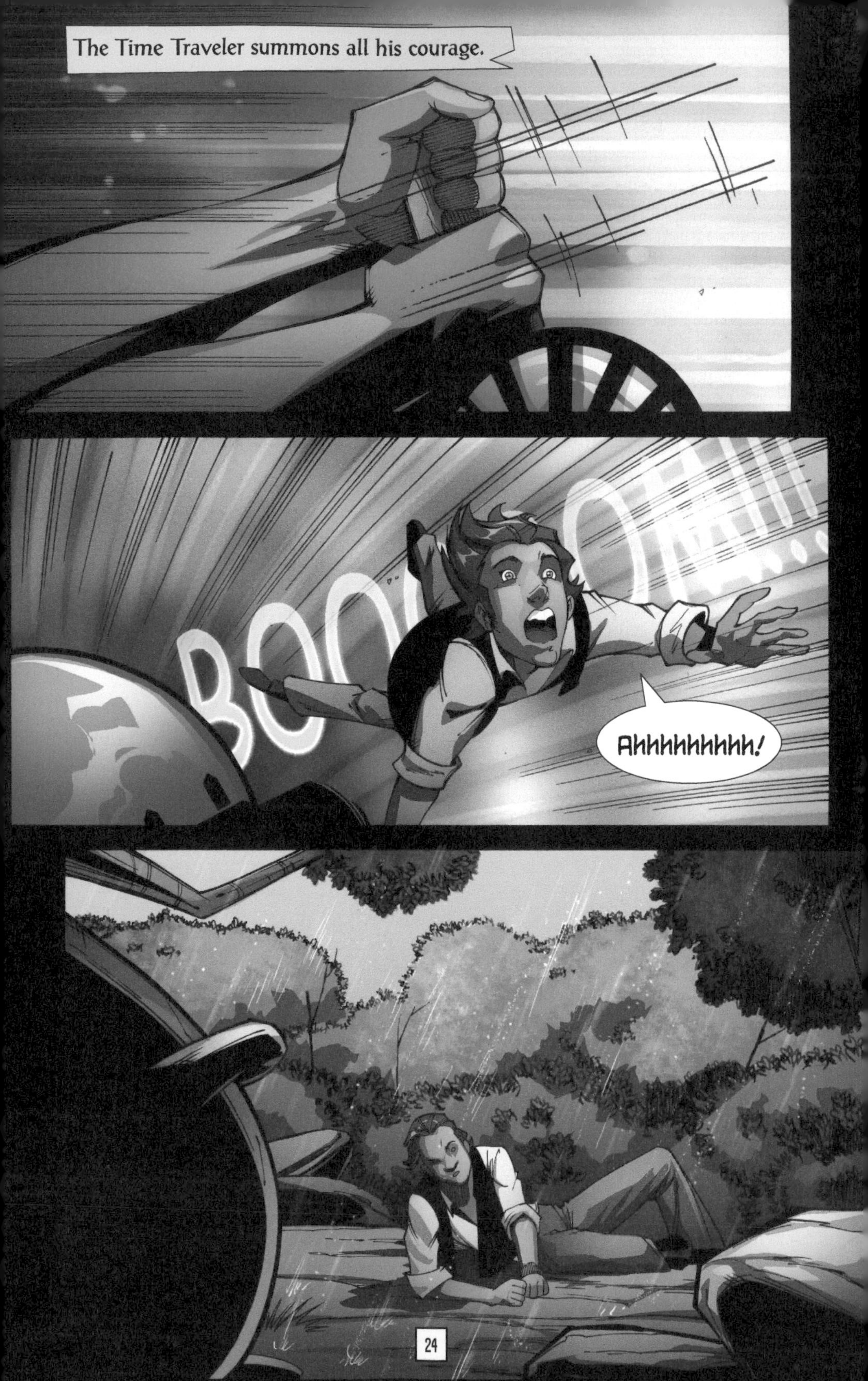
The Time Traveler summons all his courage.
Ahhhhhhhhh!

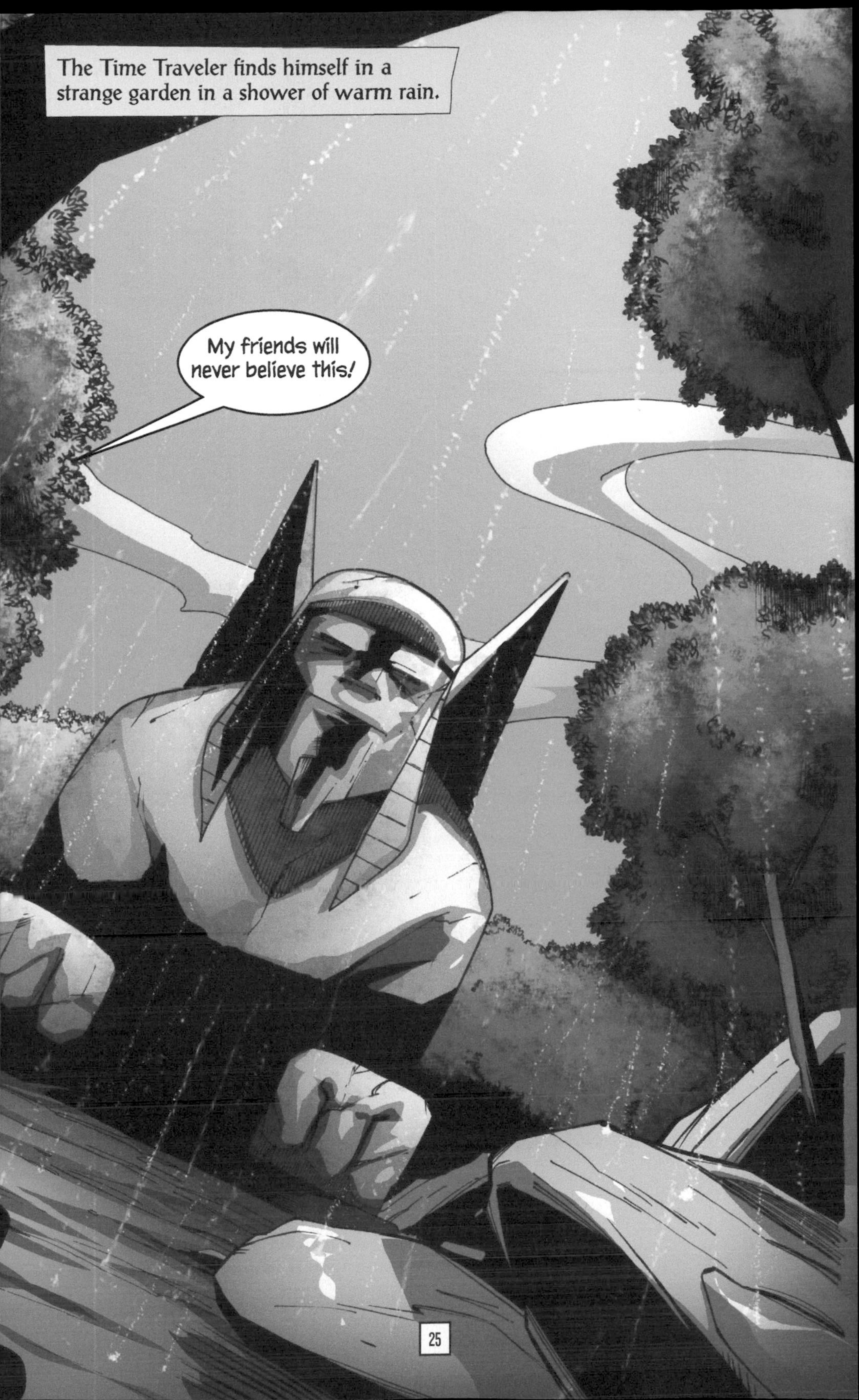
The Time Traveler finds himself in a strange garden in a shower of warm rain.
My friends will never believe this!

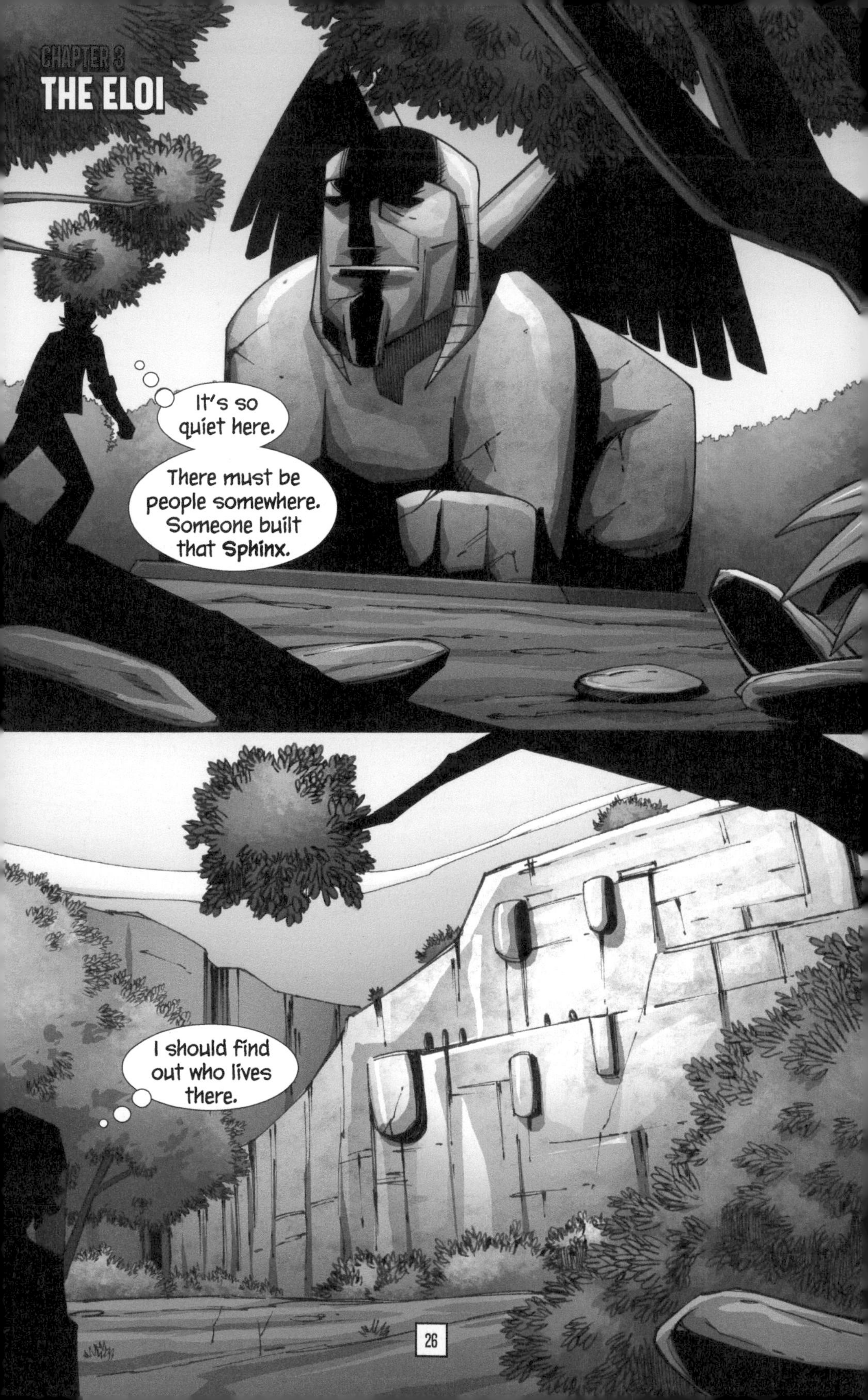
CHAPTER 3
THE ELOI
It's so quiet here.
There must be people somewhere. Someone built that Sphinx.
I should find out who lives there.

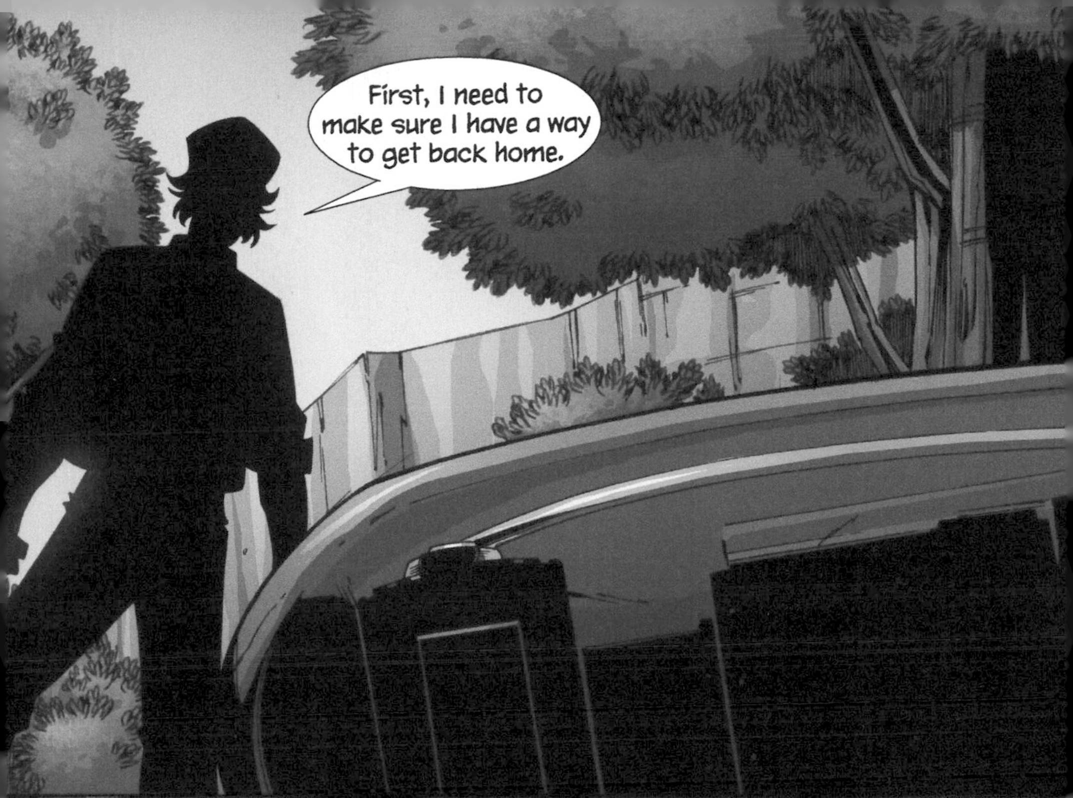
First, I need to make sure I have a way to get back home.

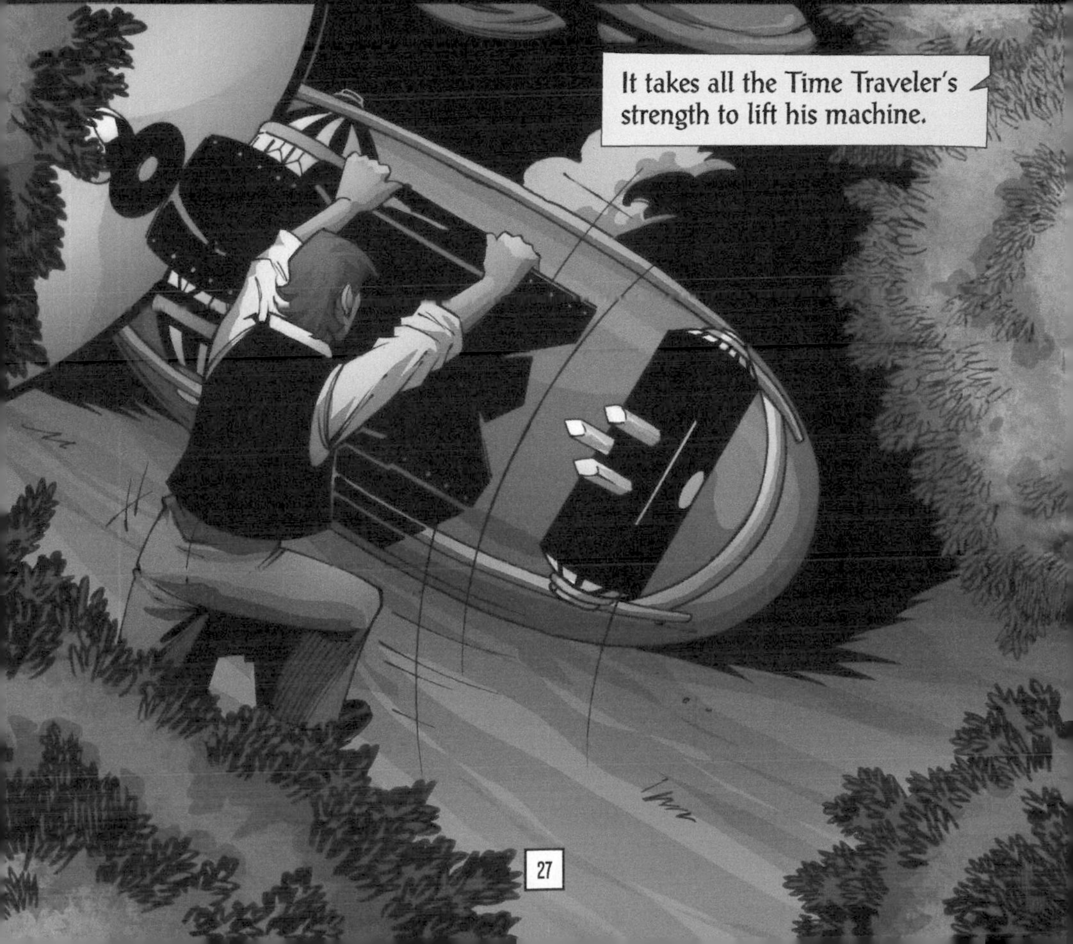
It takes all the Time Traveler's strength to lift his machine.

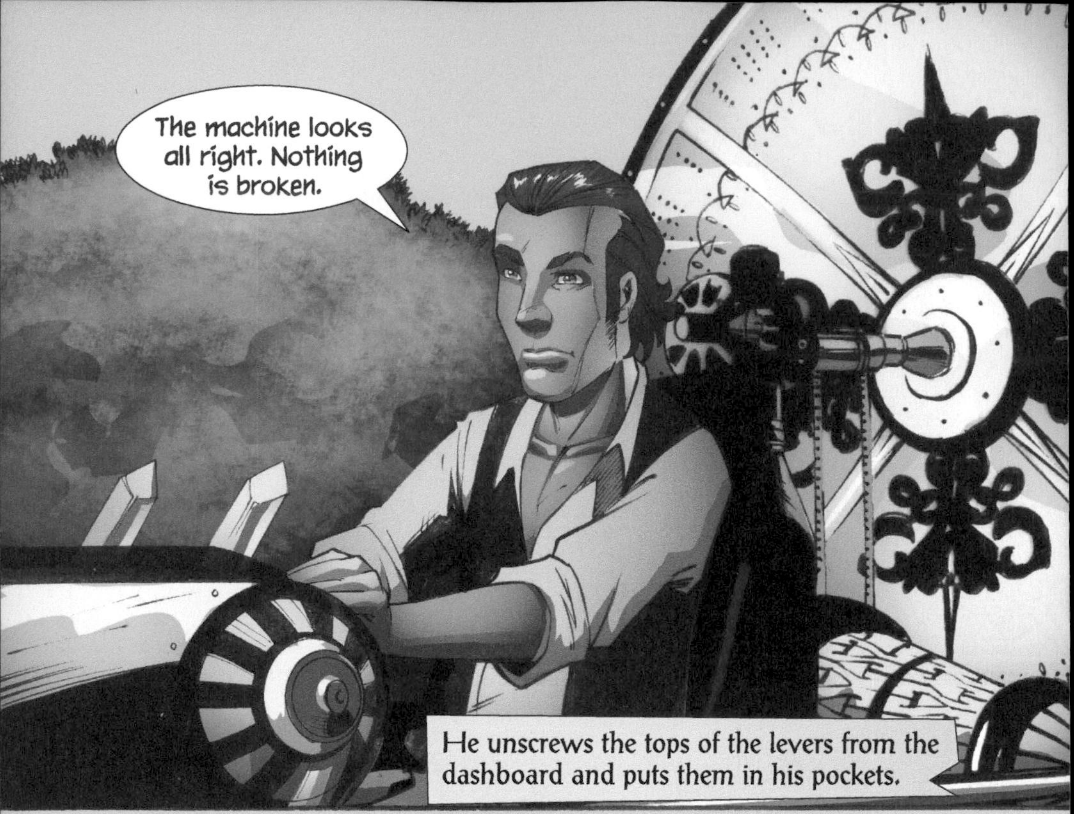
The machine looks all right. Nothing is broken.
He unscrews the tops of the levers from the dashboard and puts them in his pockets.

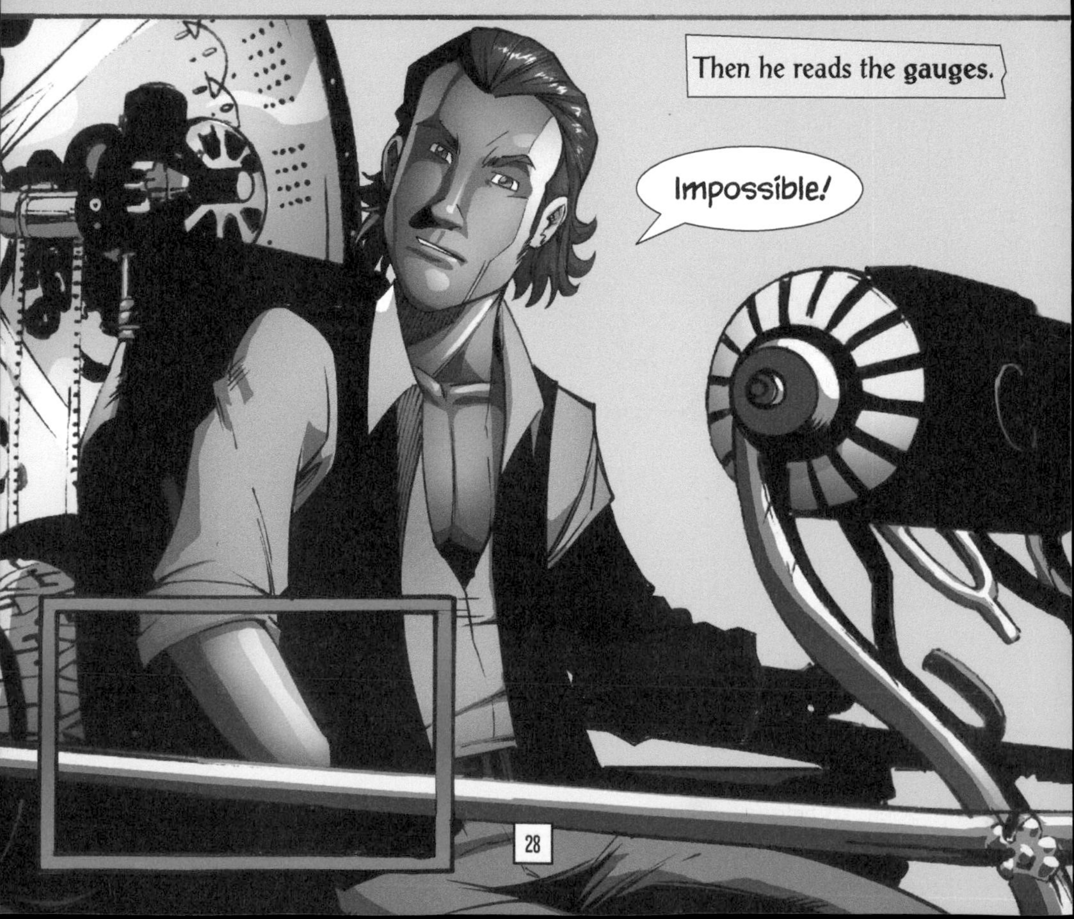
Then he reads the **gauges**.
Impossible!

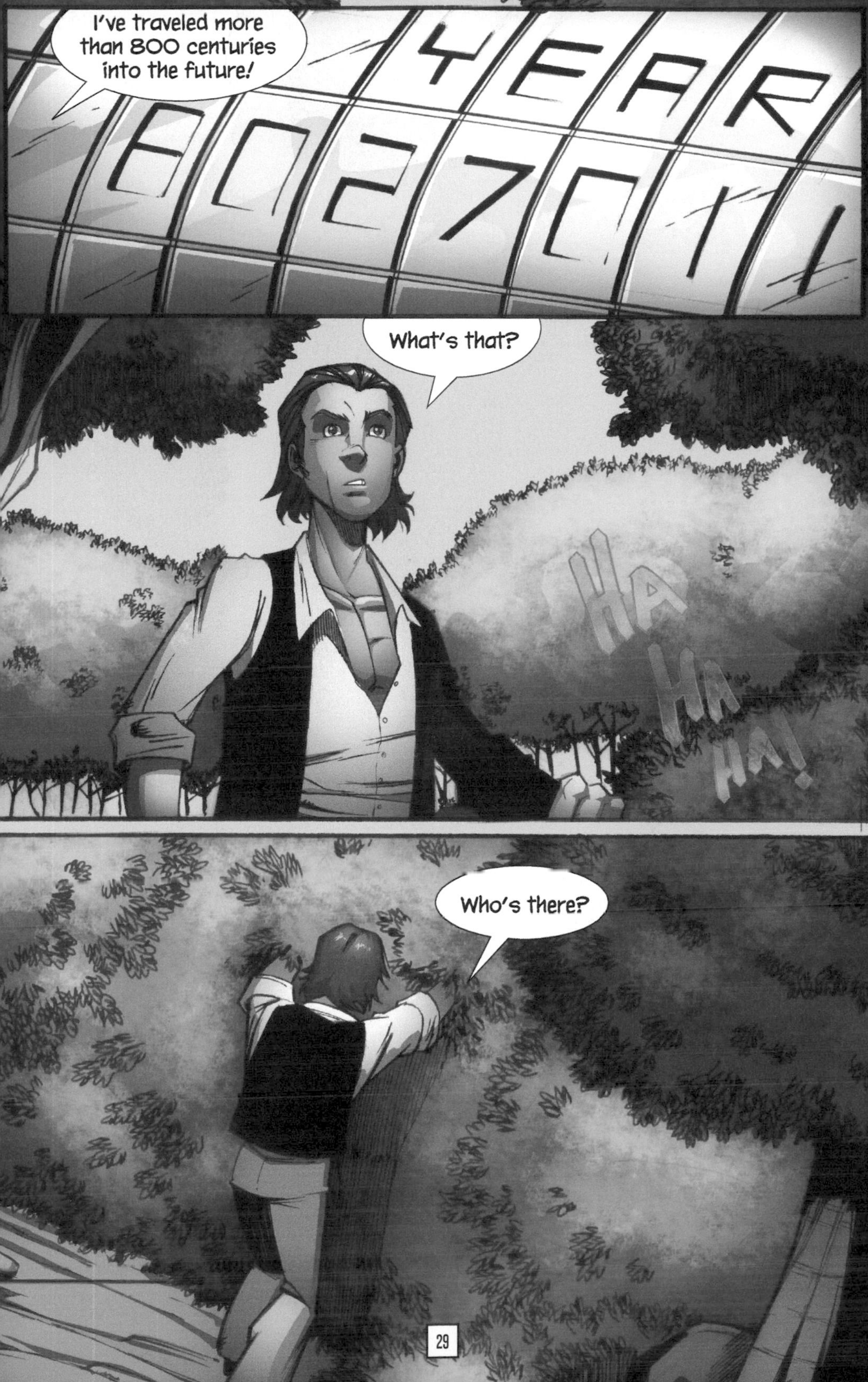
I've traveled more than 800 centuries into the future!
YEAR
802701
What's that?
HA
HA
HA!
Who's there?

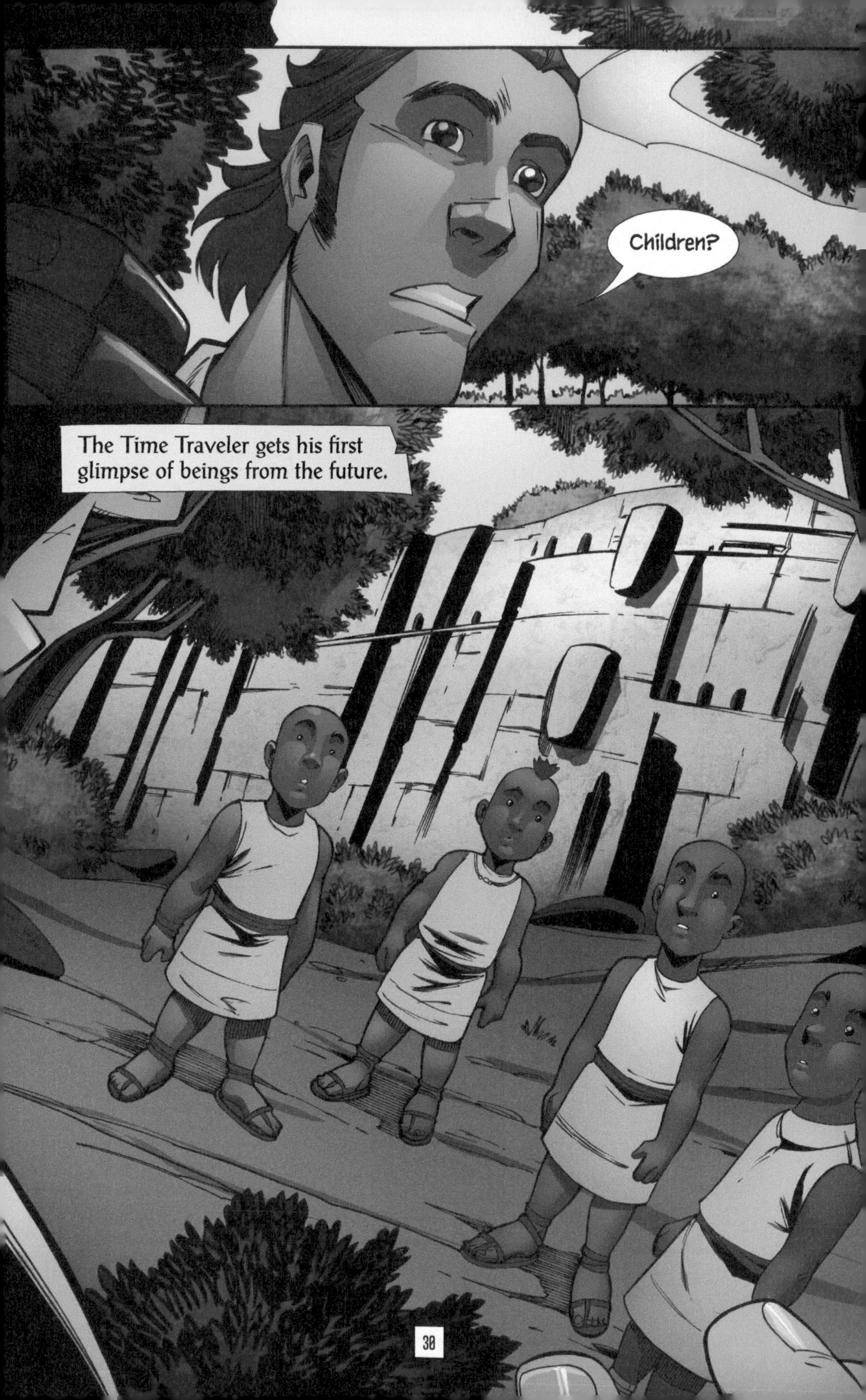
Children?
The Time Traveler gets his first glimpse of beings from the future.

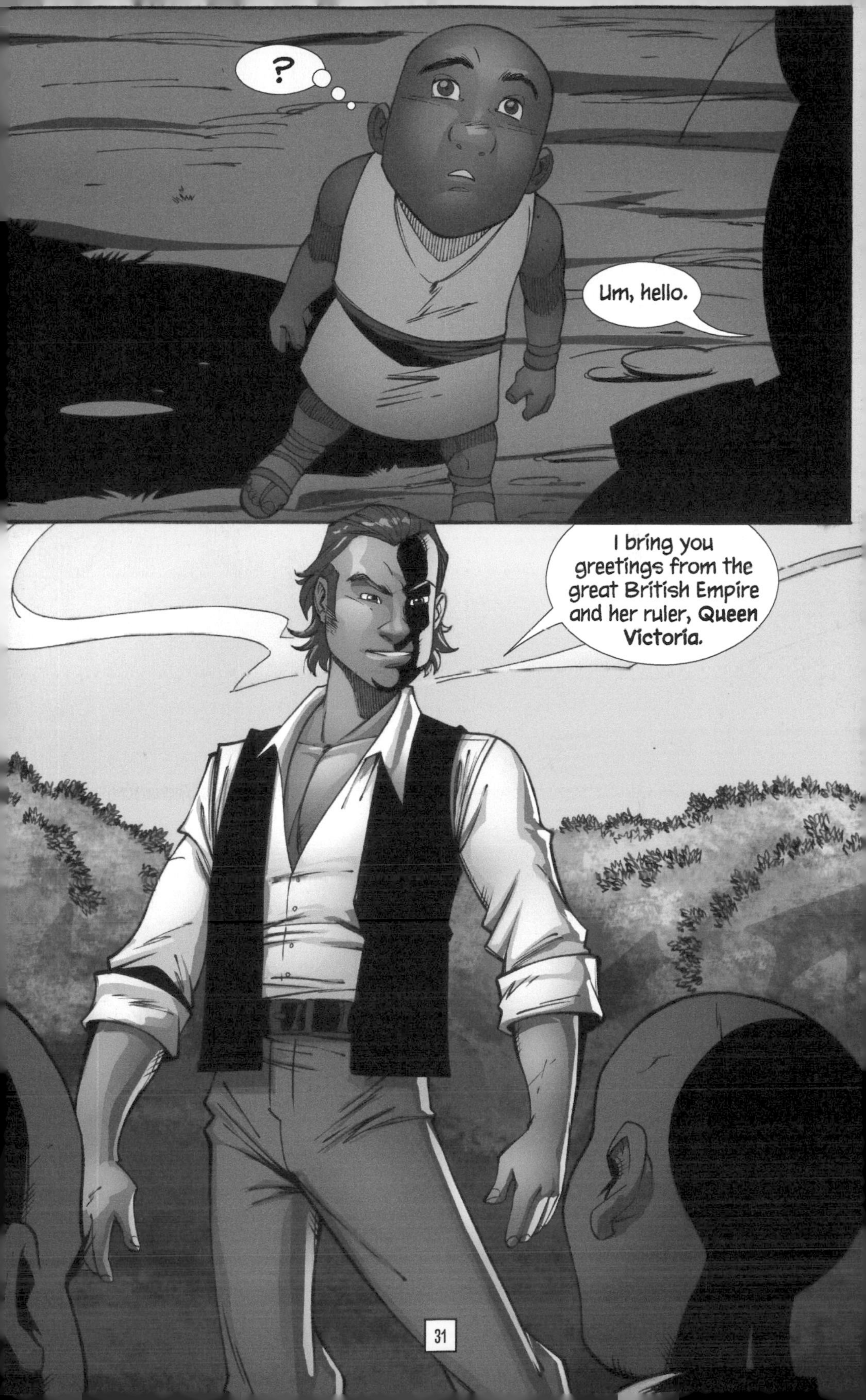
?
Um, hello.
I bring you greetings from the great British Empire and her ruler, Queen Victoria.

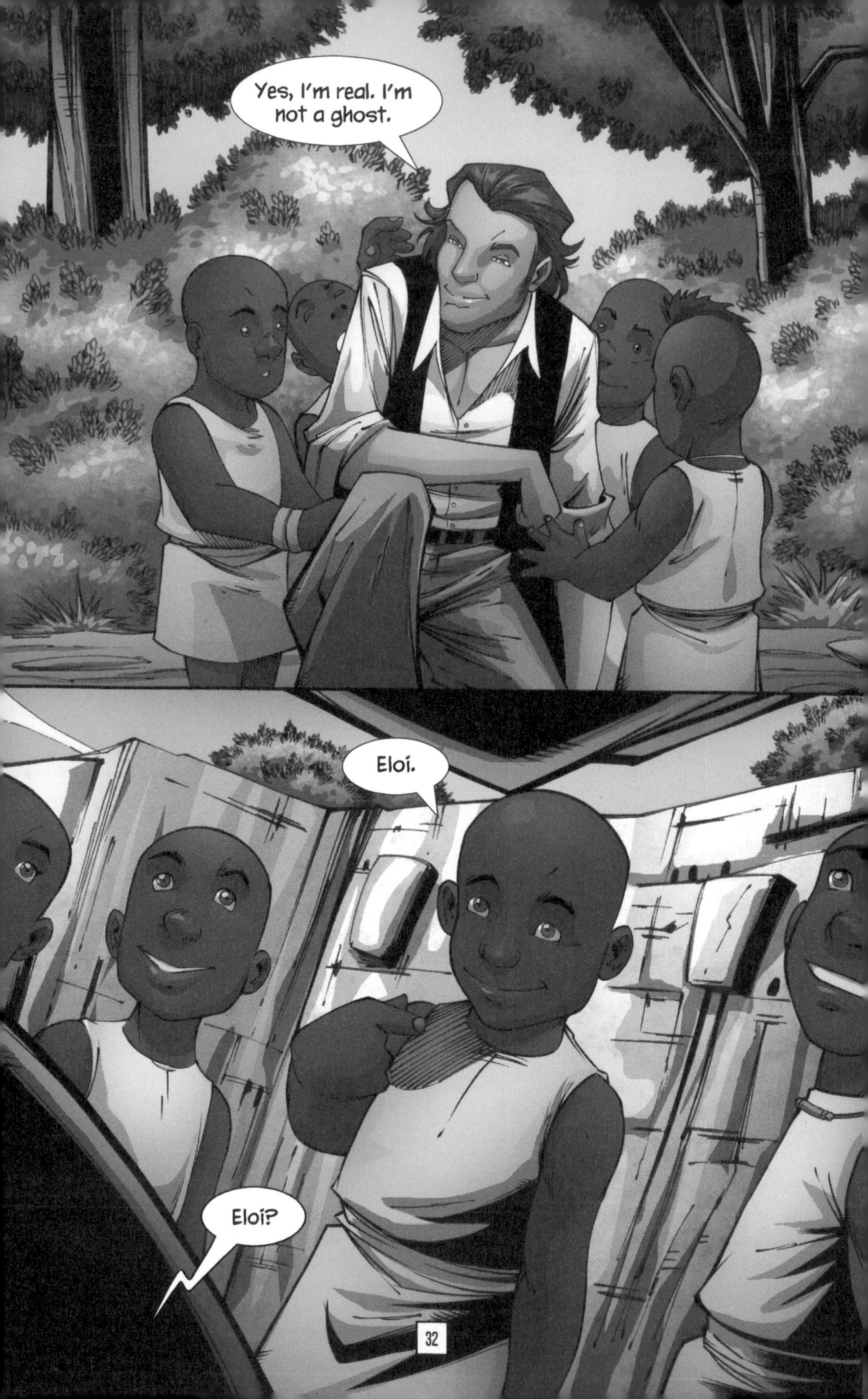
Yes, I'm real. I'm not a ghost.
Eloi.
Eloi?

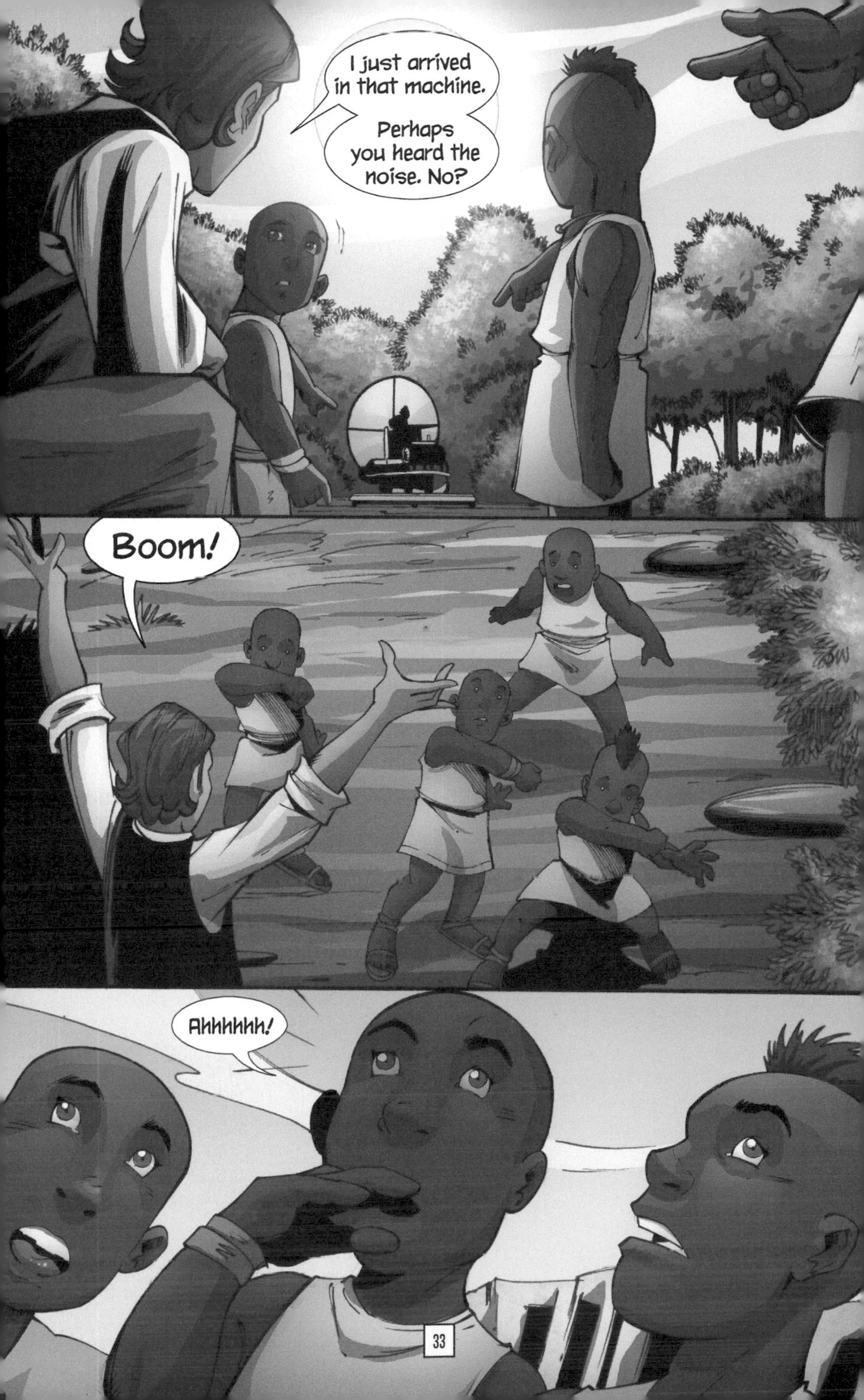
I just arrived in that machine.
Perhaps you heard the noise. No?
Boom!
Ahhhhhh!

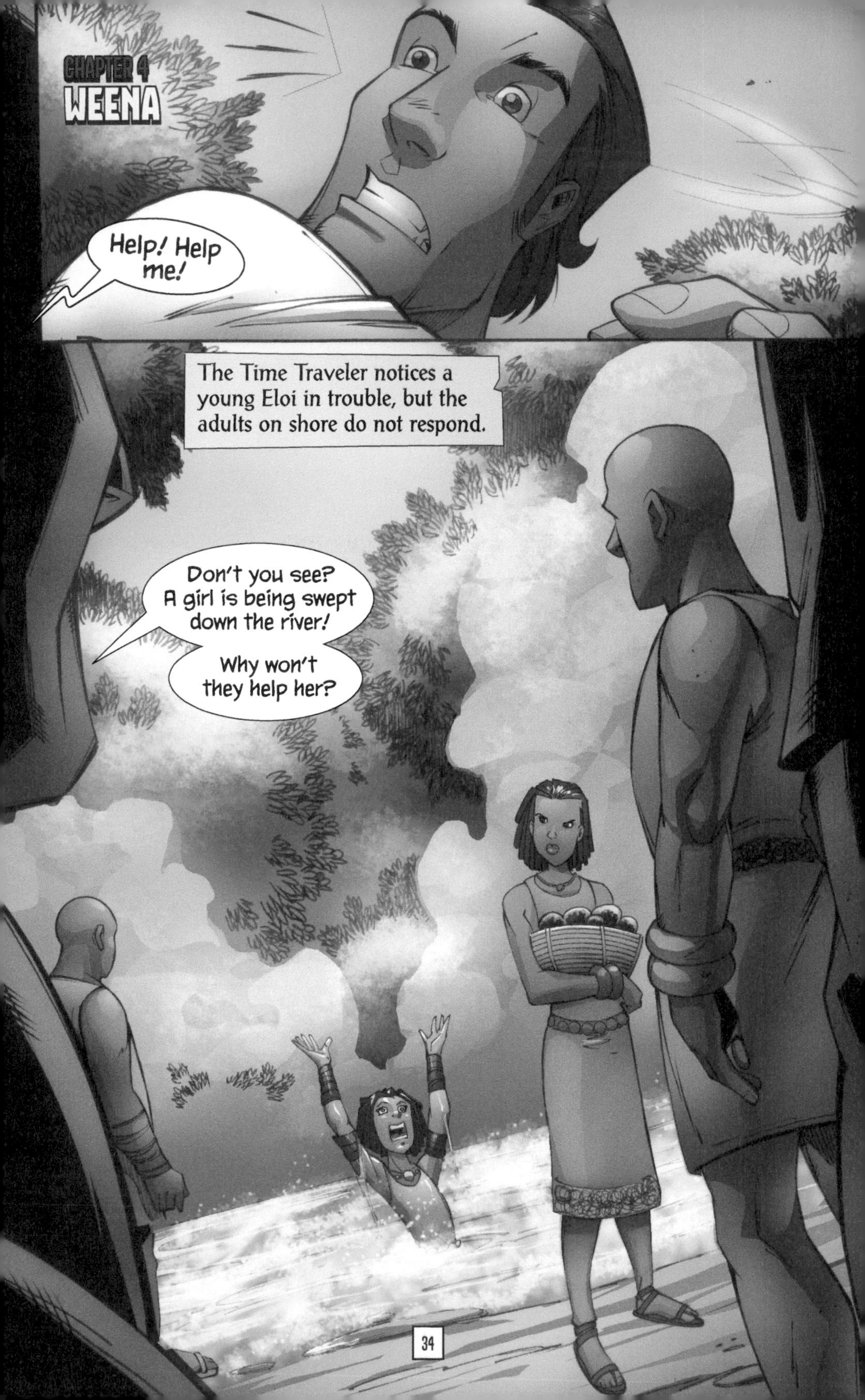
CHAPTER 4
WEENA
Help! Help me!
The Time Traveler notices a young Eloi in trouble, but the adults on shore do not respond.
Don't you see? A girl is being swept down the river!
Why won't they help her?

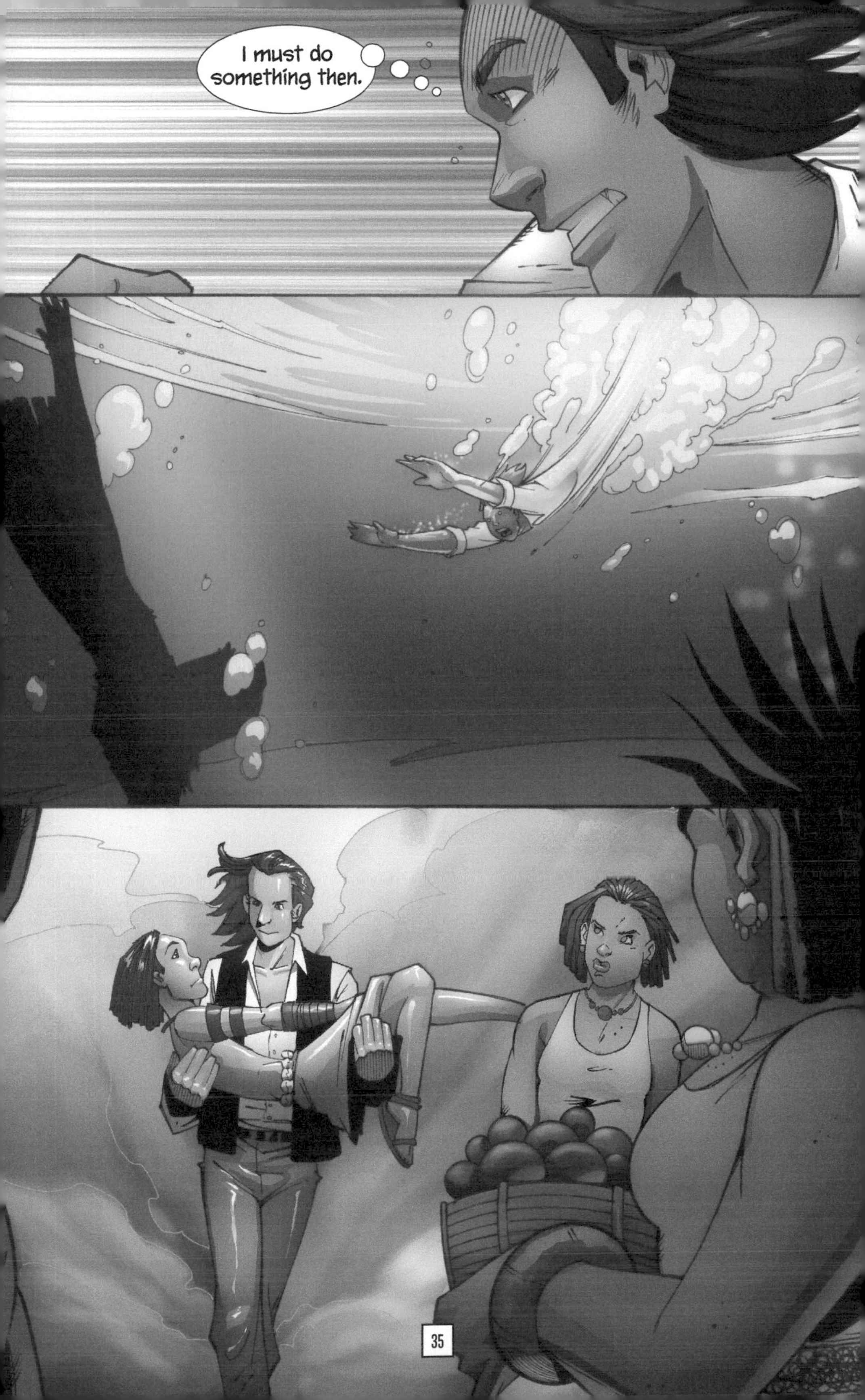
I must do something then.

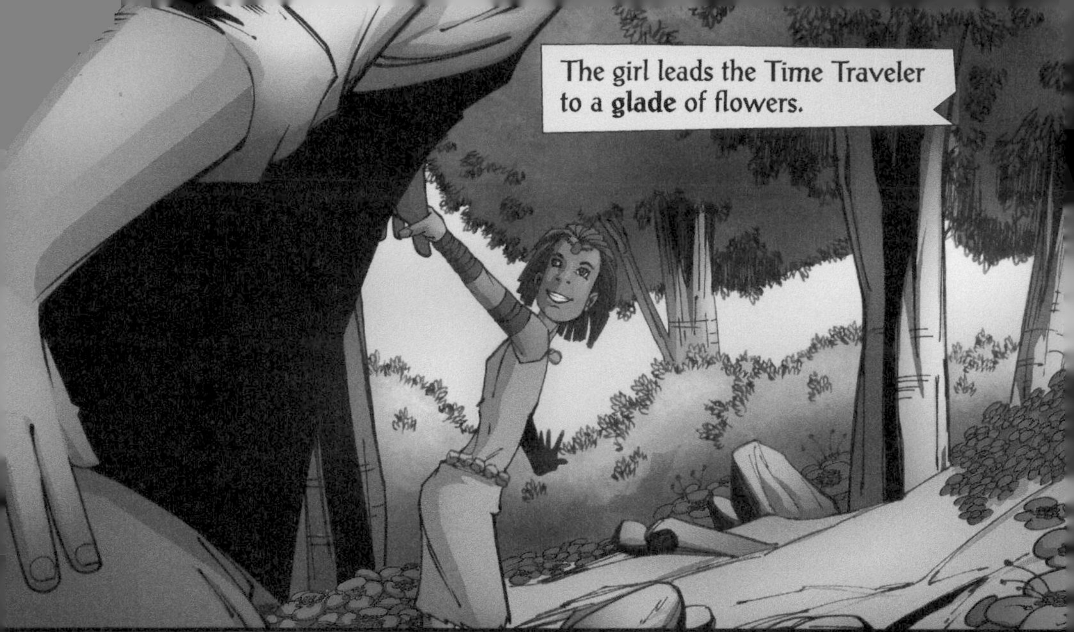
The girl leads the Time Traveler to a **glade** of flowers.

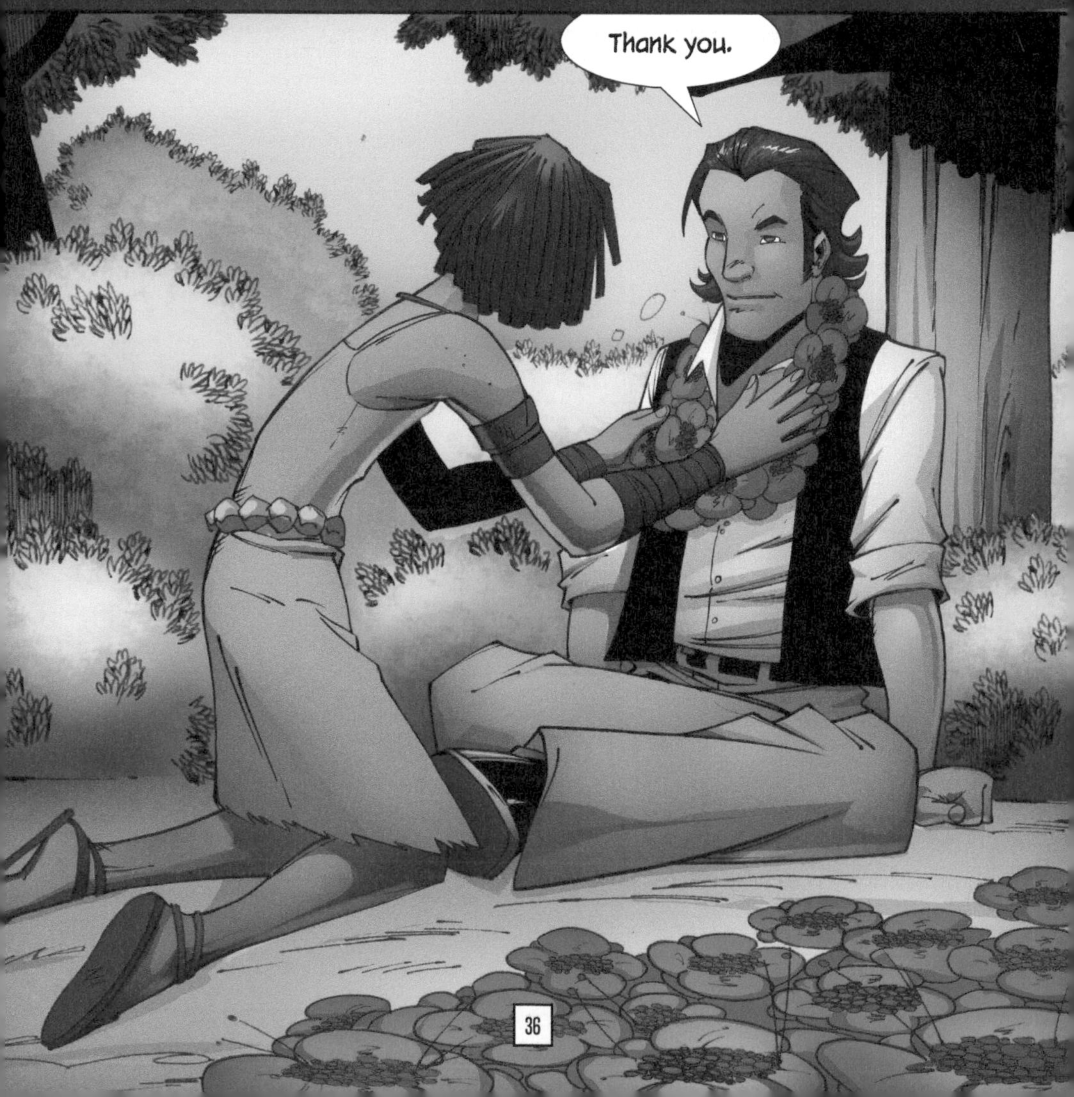
Thank you.

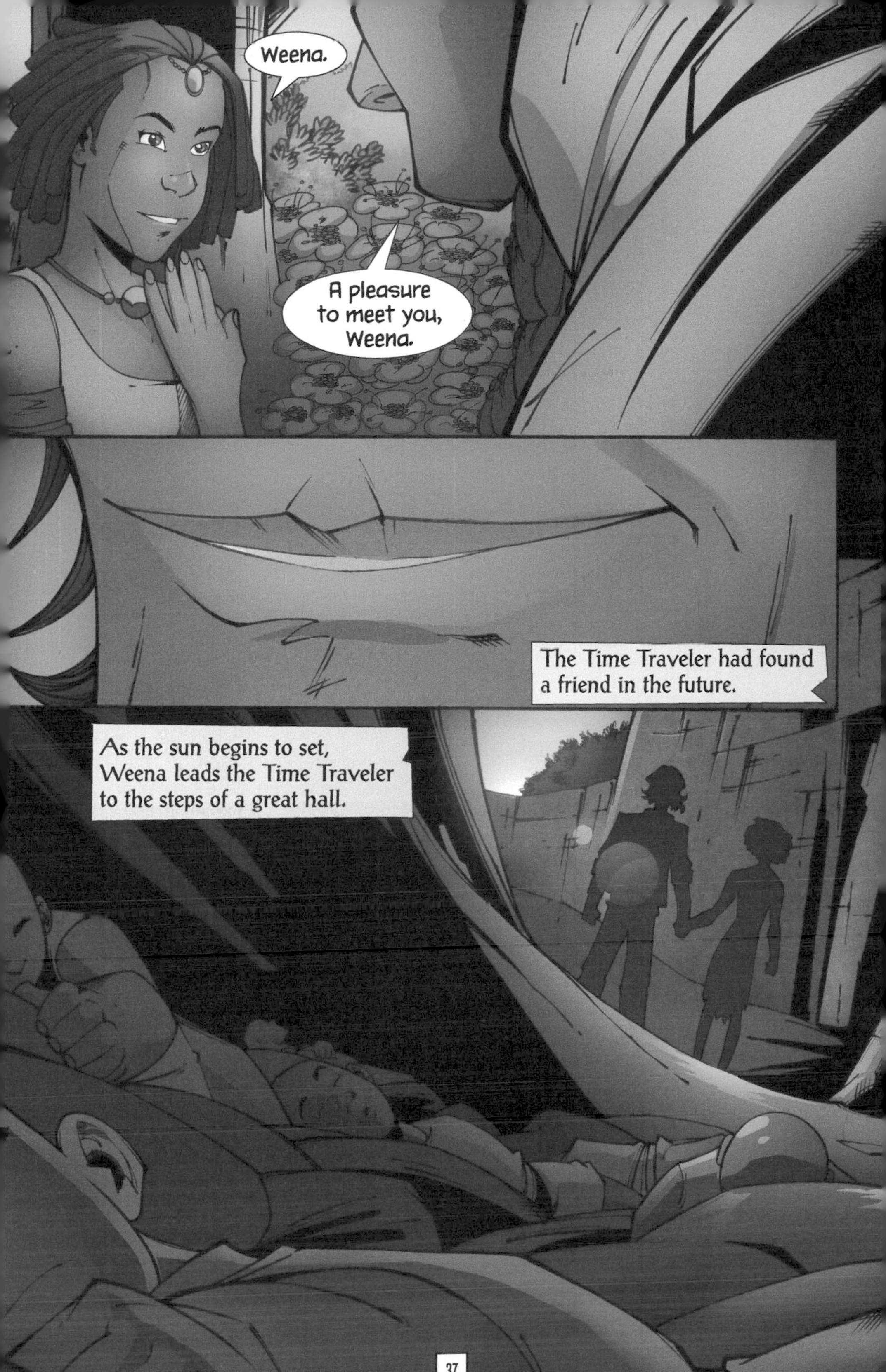

Weena.
A pleasure to meet you, Weena.
The Time Traveler had found a friend in the future.
As the sun begins to set, Weena leads the Time Traveler to the steps of a great hall.

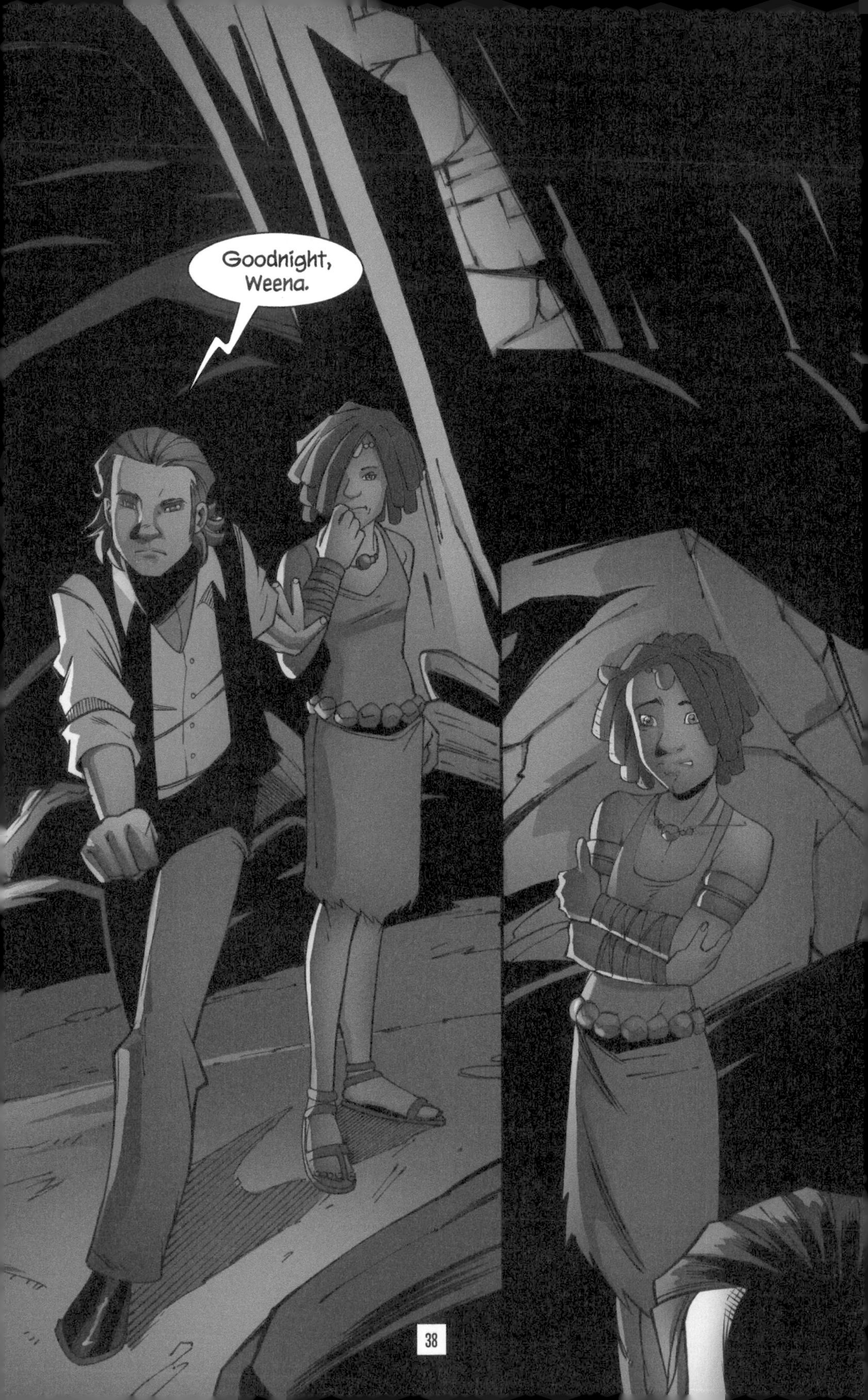
Goodnight, Weena.

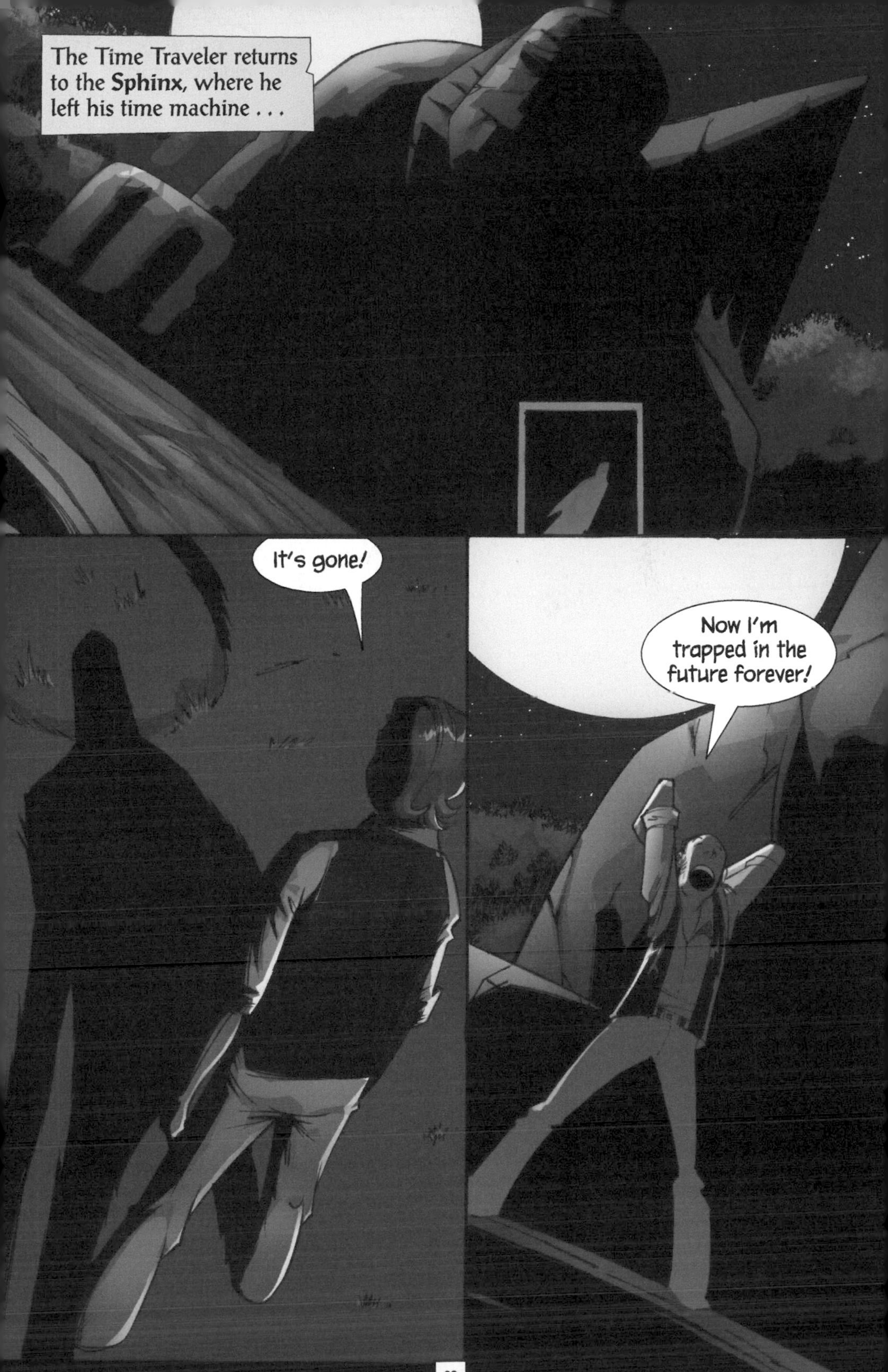

The Time Traveler returns to the **Sphinx**, where he left his time machine . . .
It's gone!
Now I'm trapped in the future forever!

CHAPTER 5

THE MORLOCKS

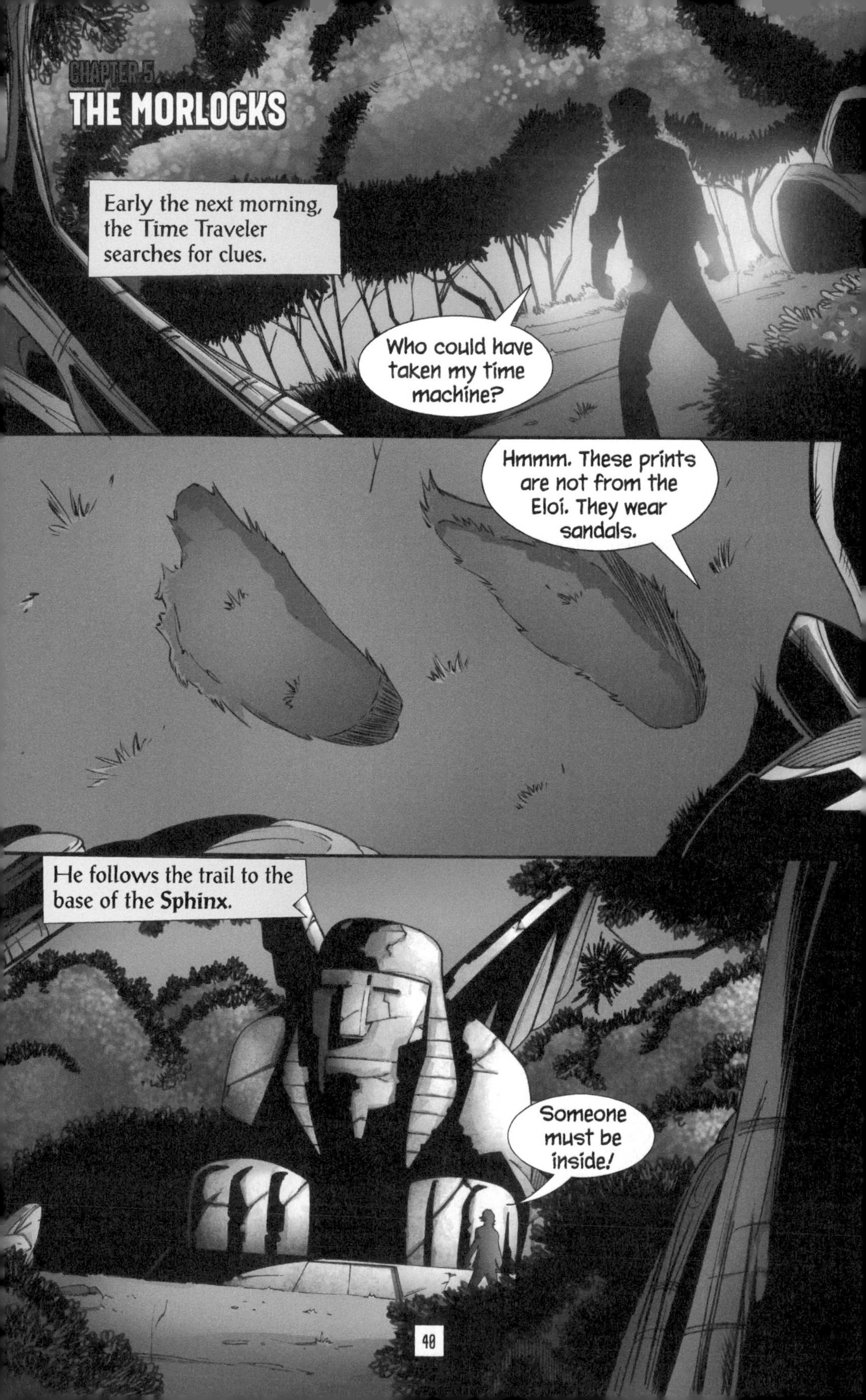

Early the next morning, the Time Traveler searches for clues.
Who could have taken my time machine?
Hmmm. These prints are not from the Eloi. They wear sandals.
He follows the trail to the base of the Sphinx.
Someone must be inside!

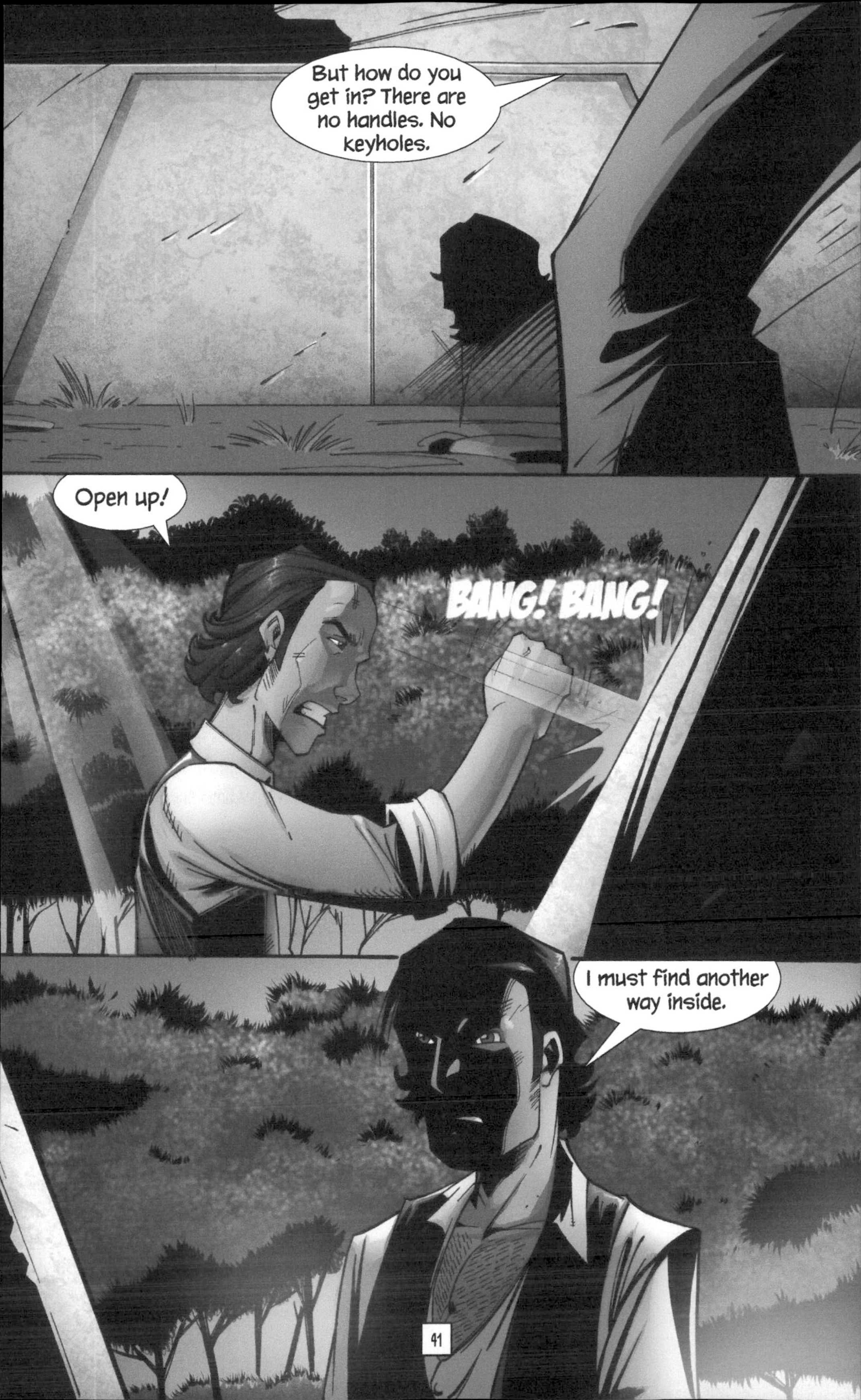
But how do you get in? There are no handles. No keyholes.
Open up!
BANG! BANG!
I must find another way inside.

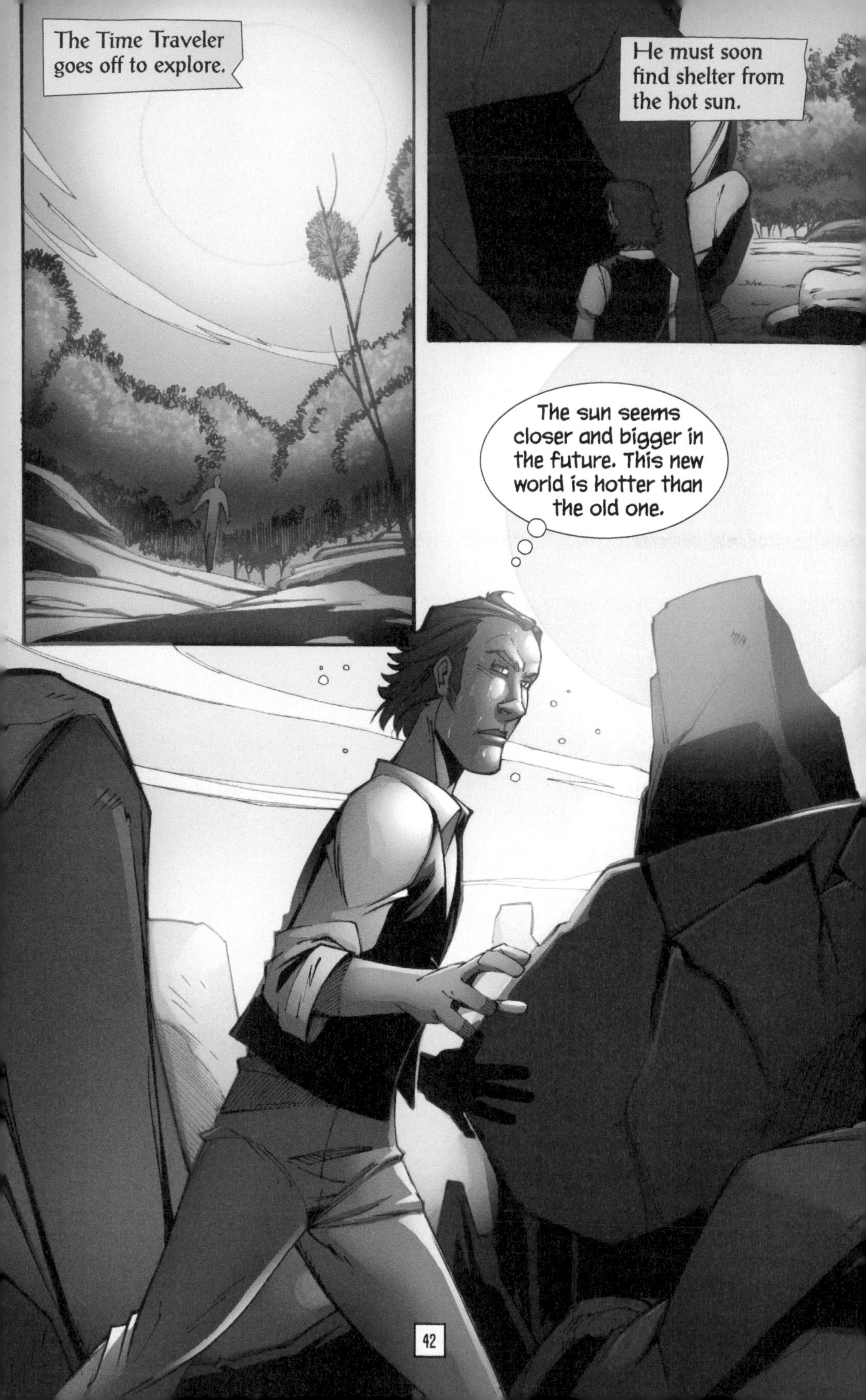
The Time Traveler goes off to explore.
He must soon find shelter from the hot sun.
The sun seems closer and bigger in the future. This new world is hotter than the old one.

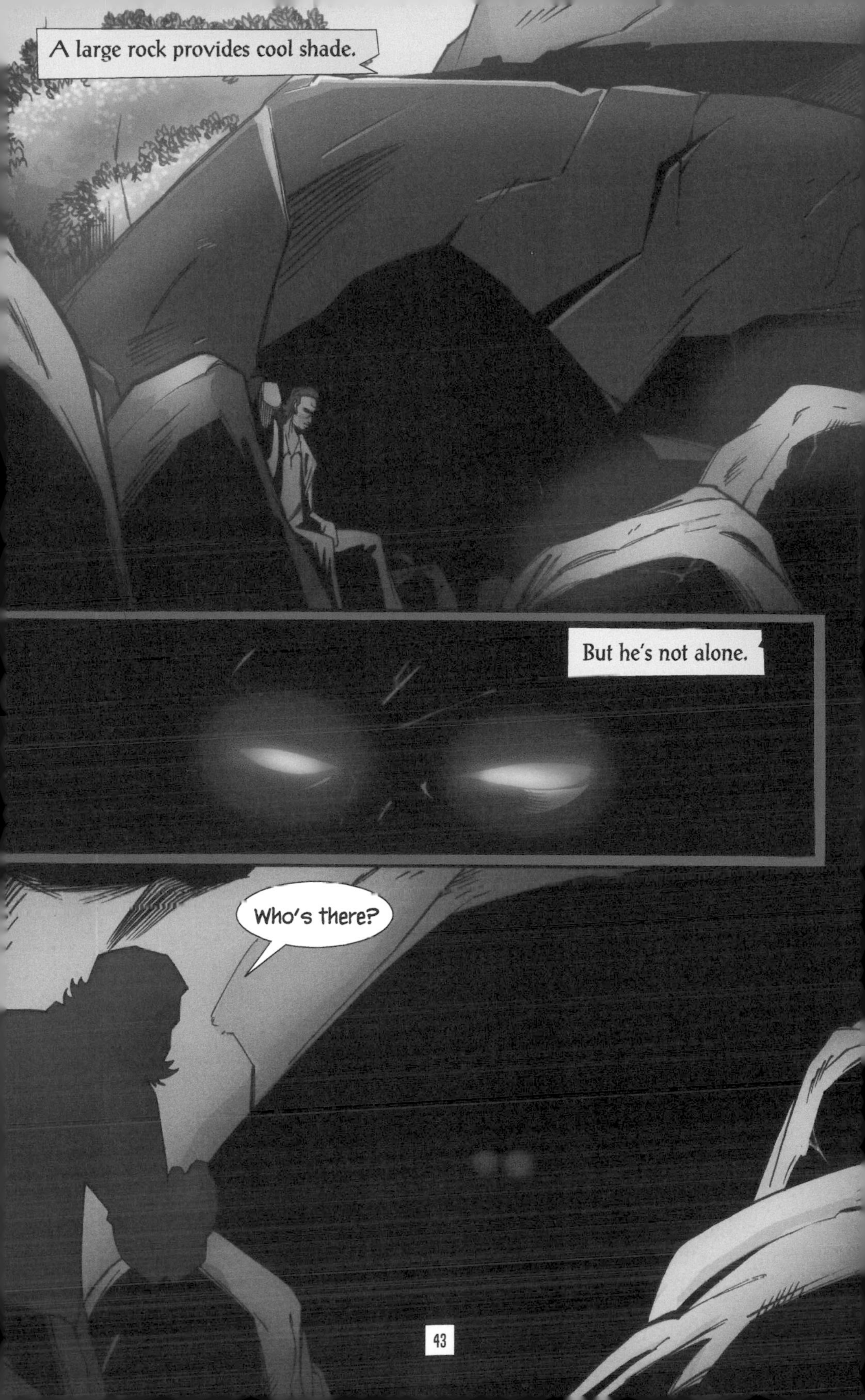
A large rock provides cool shade.
But he's not alone.
Who's there?

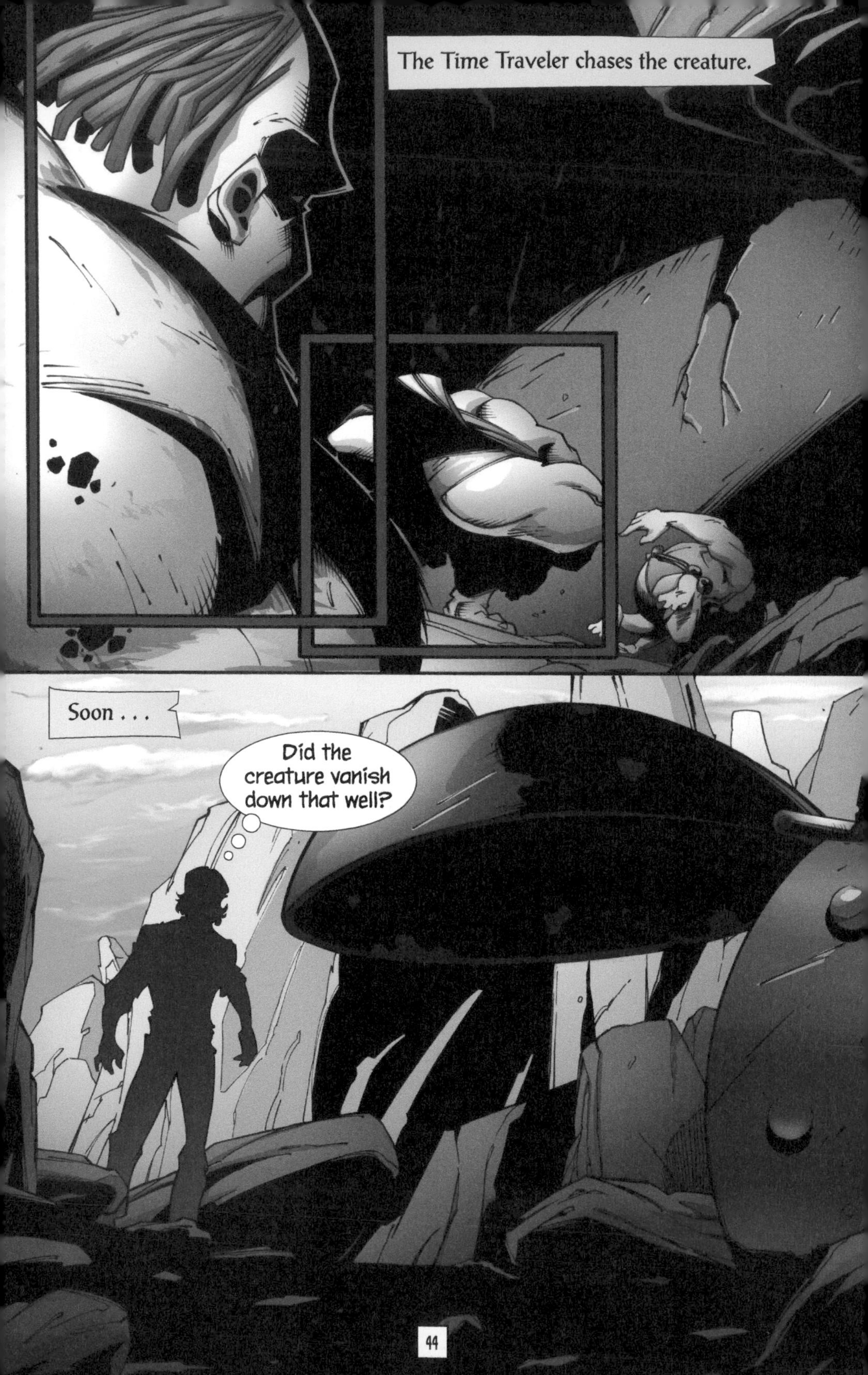
The Time Traveler chases the creature.
Soon . . .
Did the creature vanish down that well?

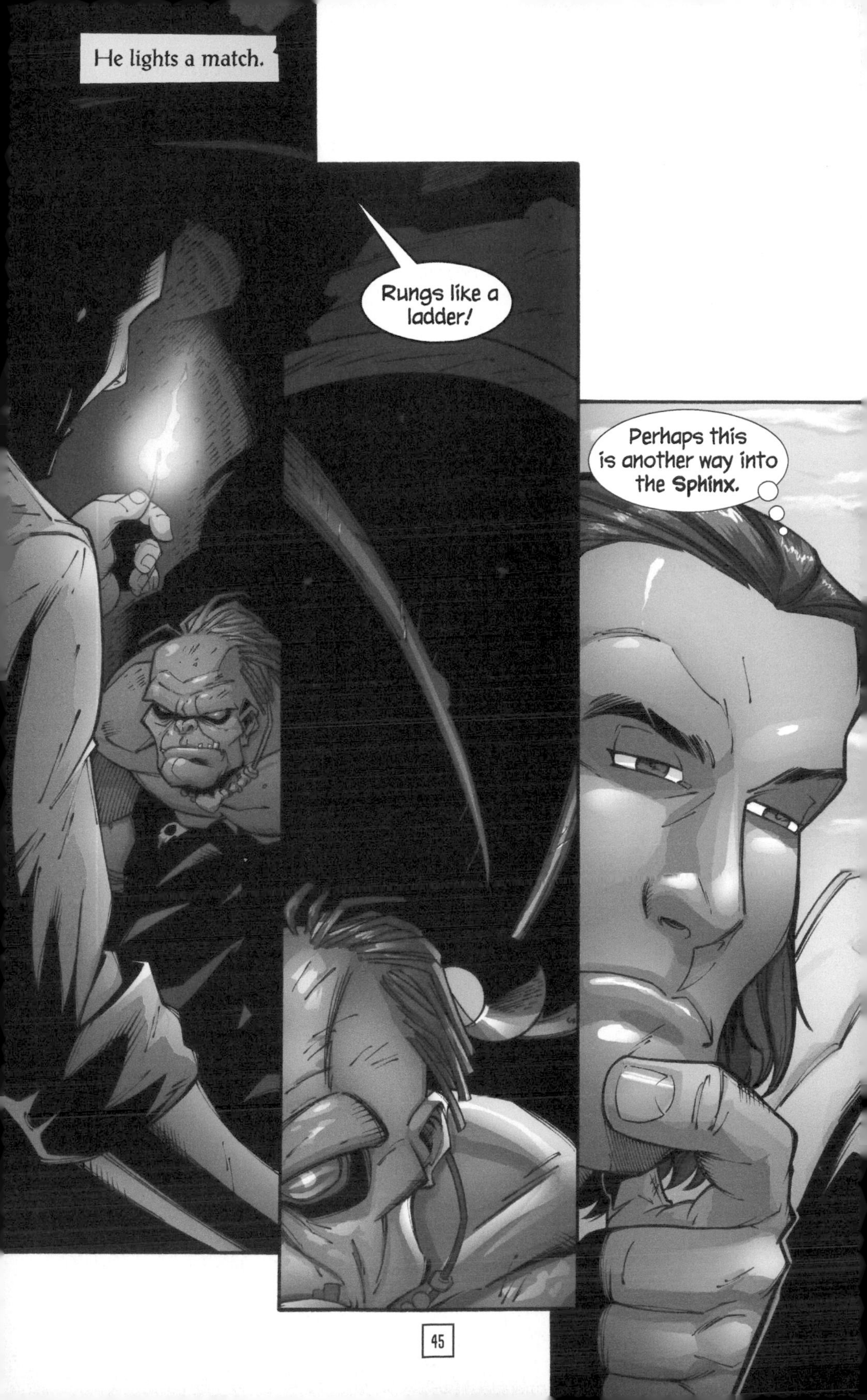
He lights a match.
Rungs like a ladder!
Perhaps this is another way into the Sphinx.

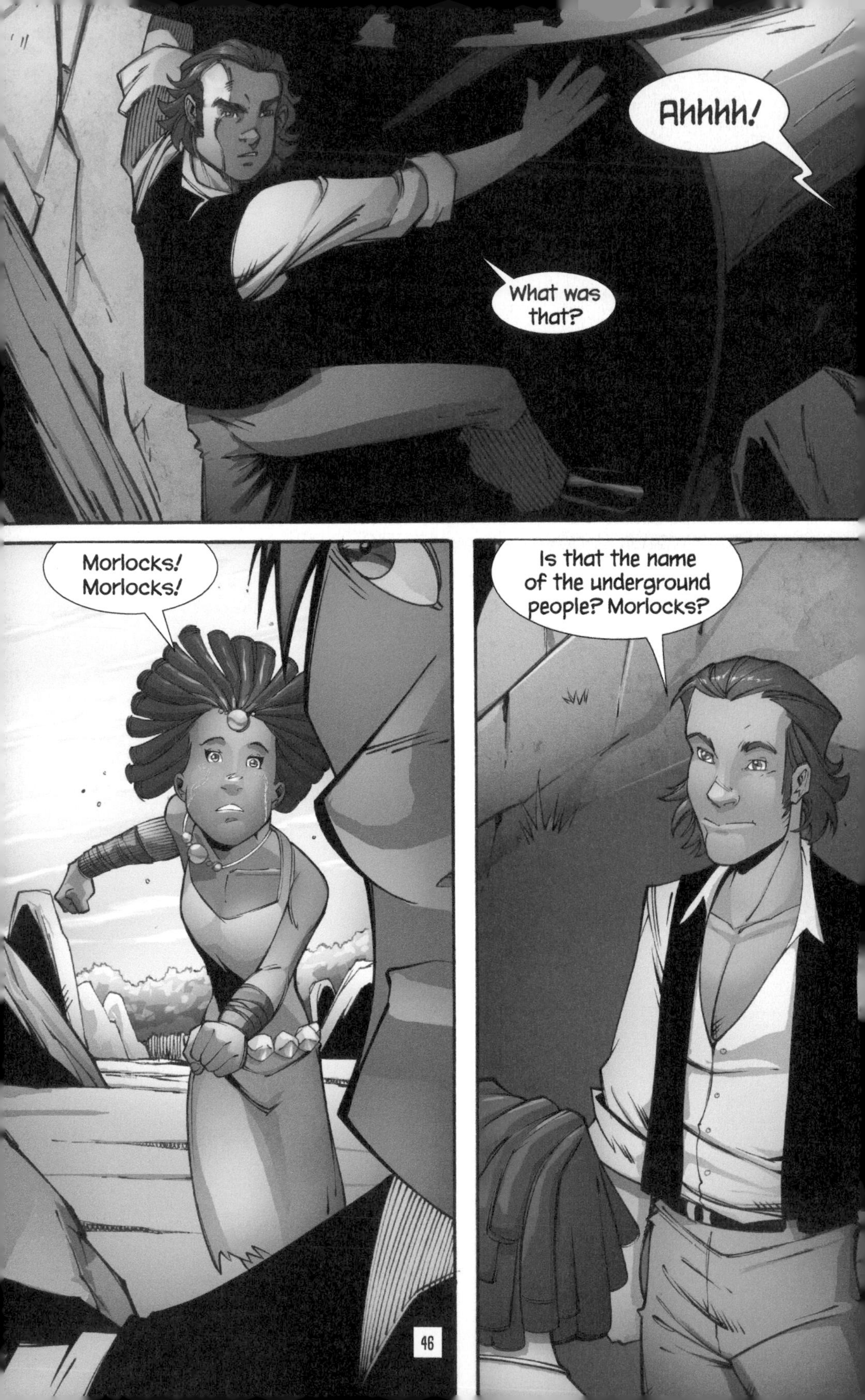
Ahhhh!
What was that?
Morlocks! Morlocks!
Is that the name of the underground people? Morlocks?

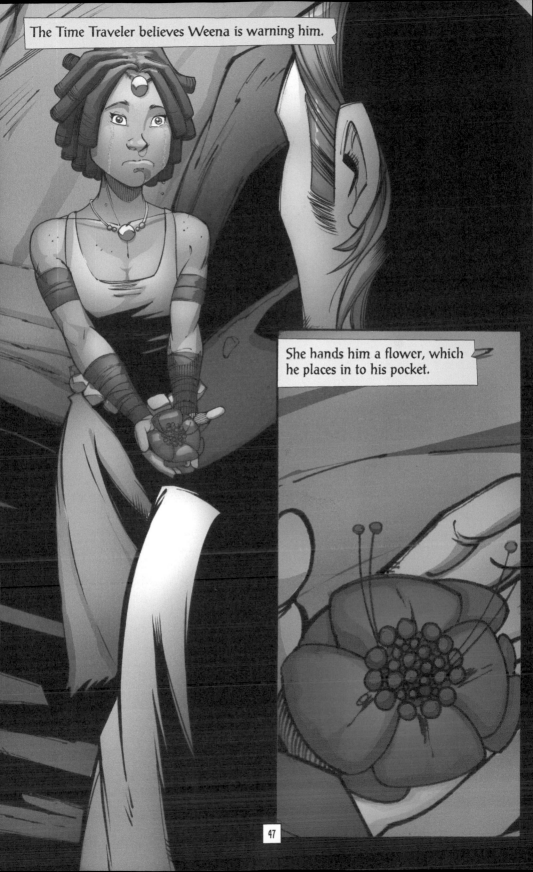

The Time Traveler believes Weena is warning him.

She hands him a flower, which he places in to his pocket.

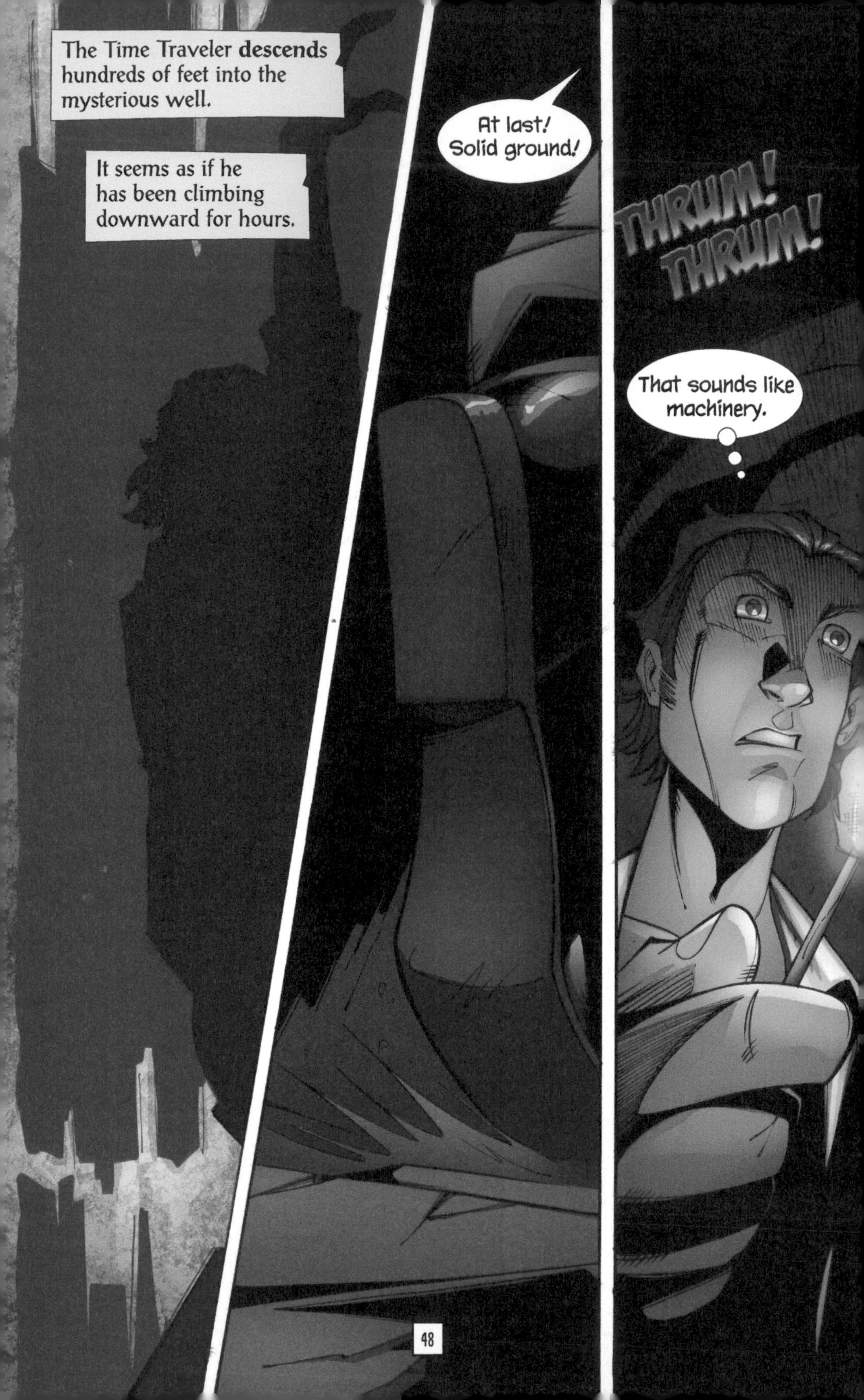

The Time Traveler **descends** hundreds of feet into the mysterious well.
It seems as if he has been climbing downward for hours.
At last! Solid ground!
THRUM! THRUM!
That sounds like machinery.

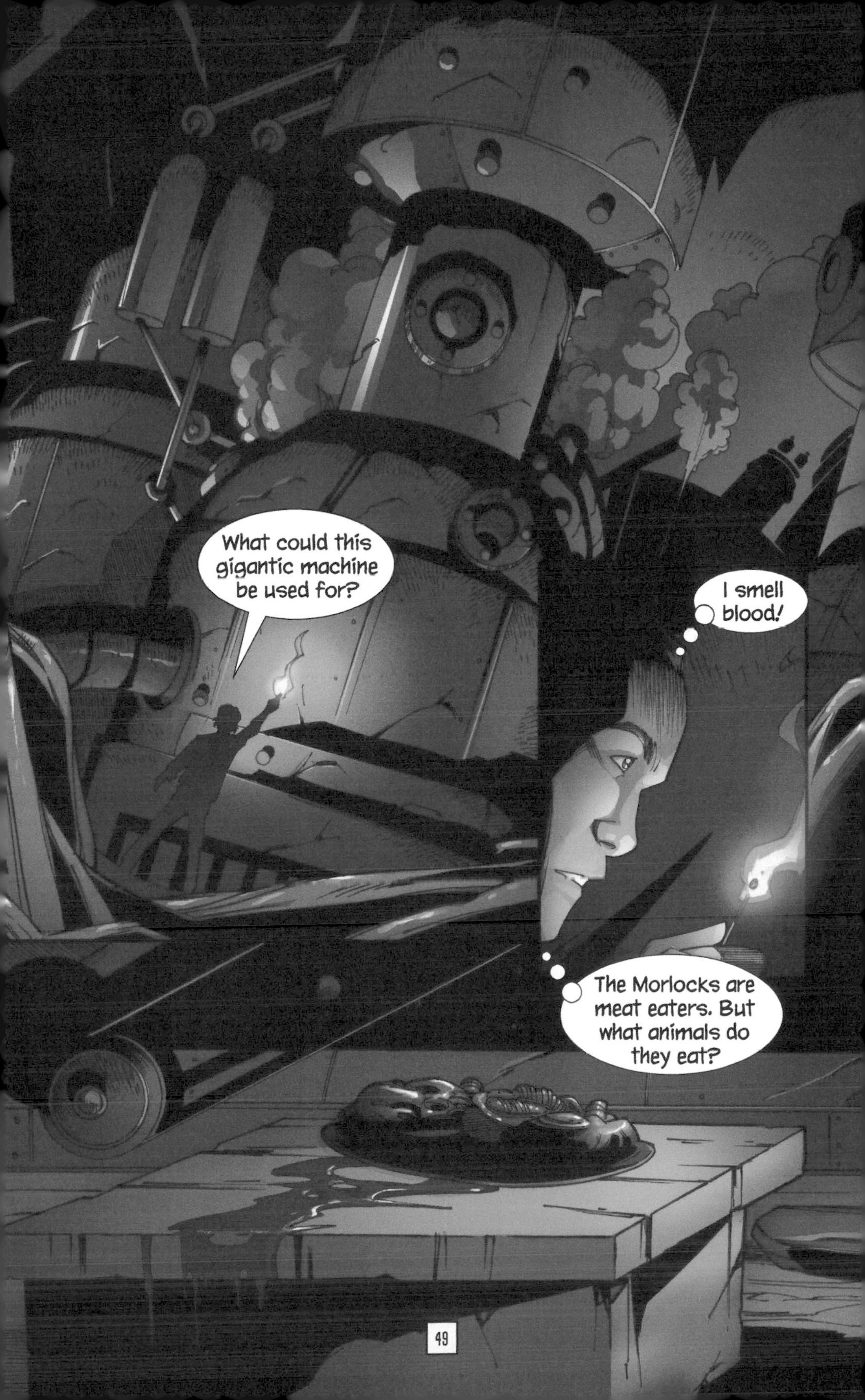
What could this gigantic machine be used for?
I smell blood!
The Morlocks are meat eaters. But what animals do they eat?

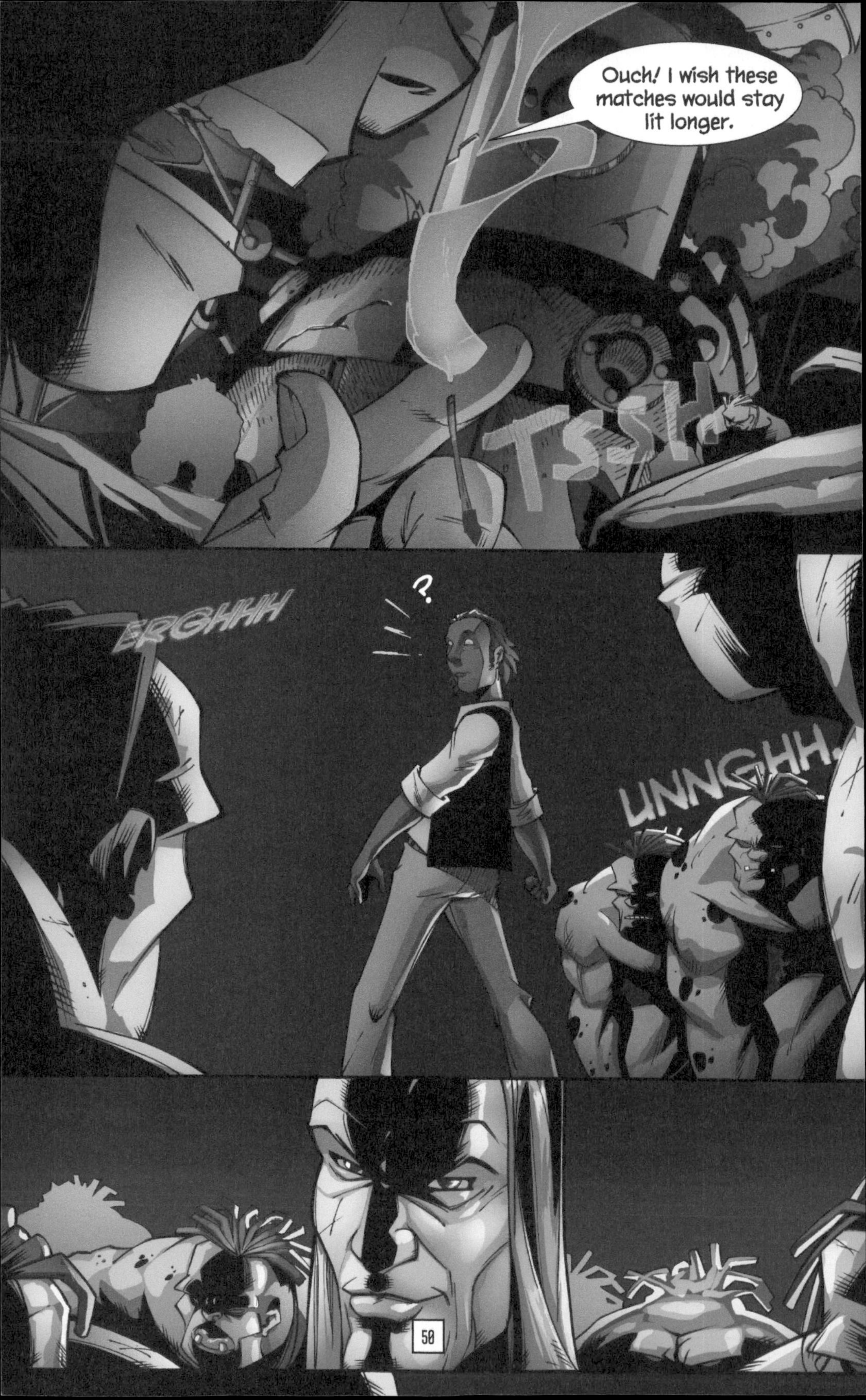
Ouch! I wish these matches would stay lit longer.
TSSH
?
ERGHHH
UNNGHH

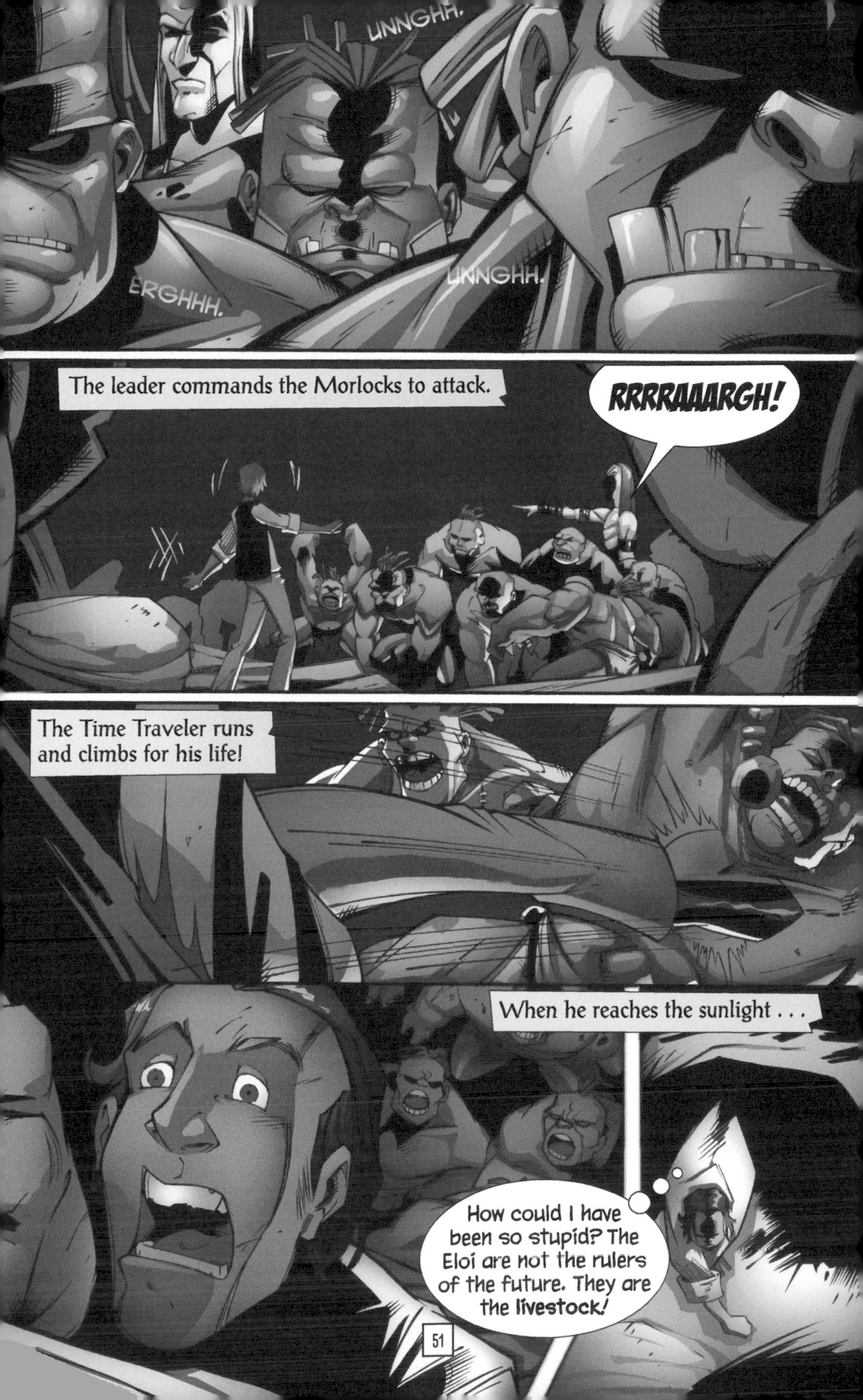
UNNGHH.
ERGHHH.
UNNGHH.
The leader commands the Morlocks to attack.
RRRRAAAARGH!
The Time Traveler runs and climbs for his life!
When he reaches the sunlight . . .
How could I have been so stupid? The Eloi are not the rulers of the future. They are the livestock!

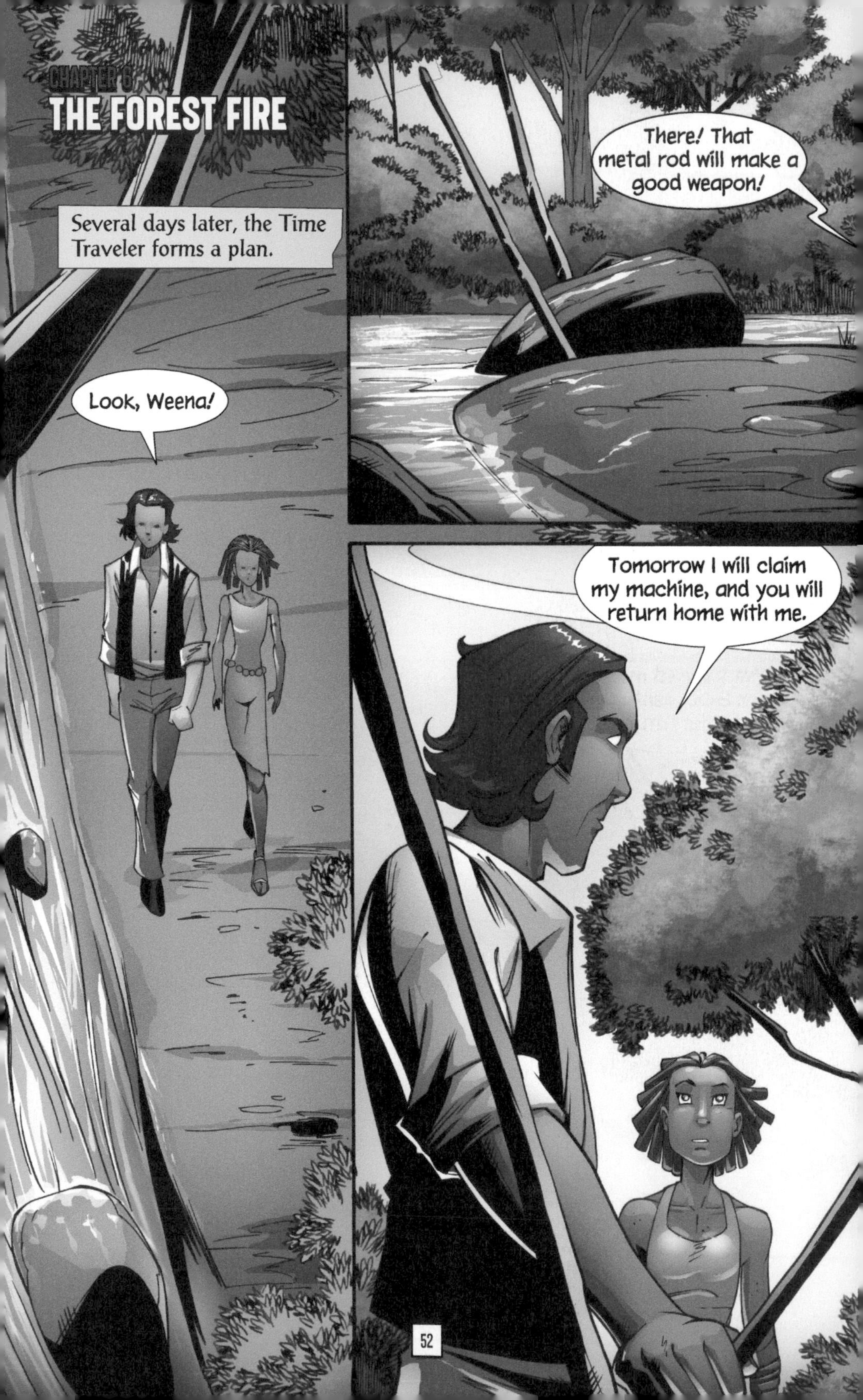
CHAPTER 6
THE FOREST FIRE
Several days later, the Time Traveler forms a plan.
Look, Weena!
There! That metal rod will make a good weapon!
Tomorrow I will claim my machine, and you will return home with me.

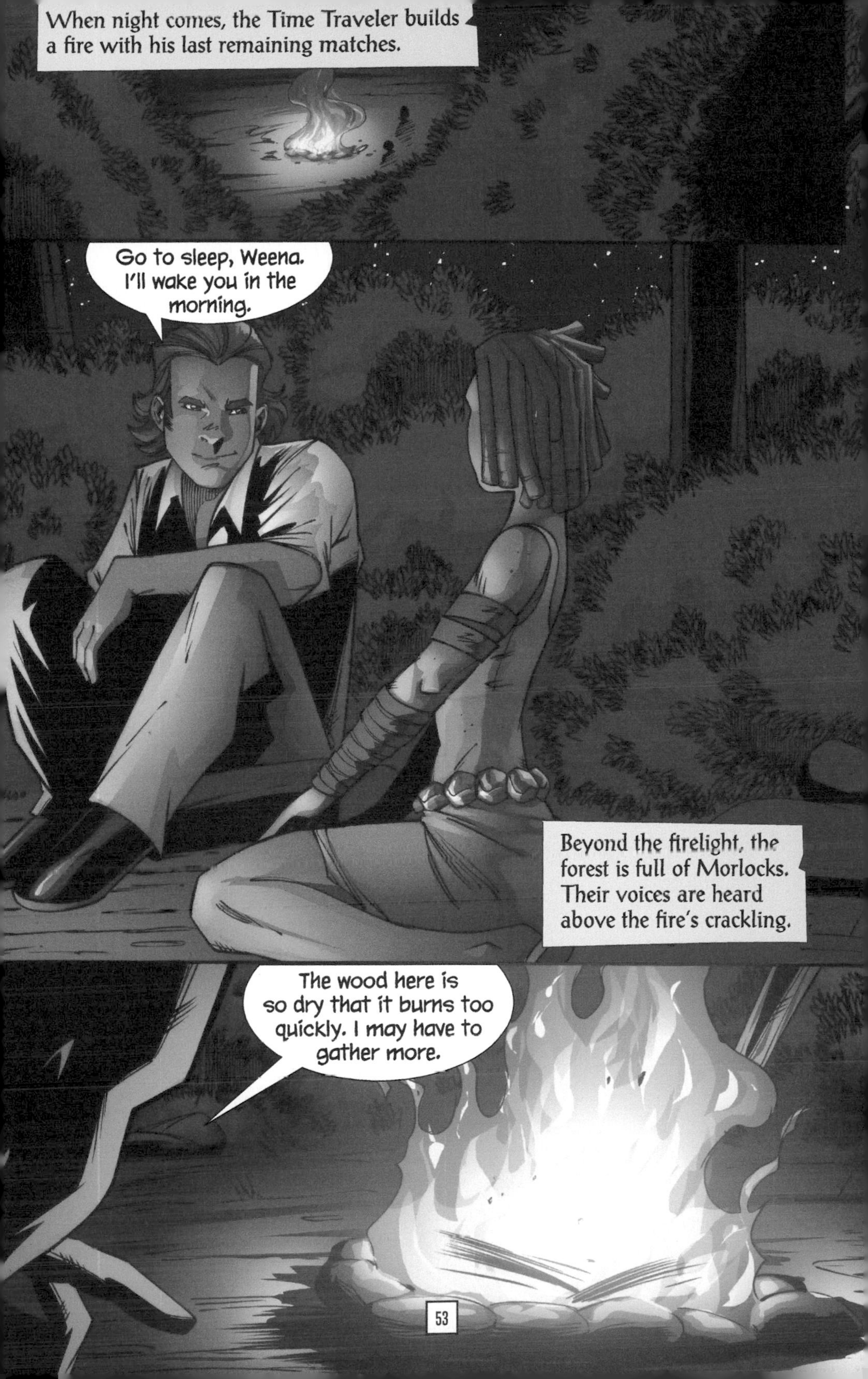

When night comes, the Time Traveler builds a fire with his last remaining matches.
Go to sleep, Weena. I'll wake you in the morning.
Beyond the firelight, the forest is full of Morlocks. Their voices are heard above the fire's crackling.
The wood here is so dry that it burns too quickly. I may have to gather more.

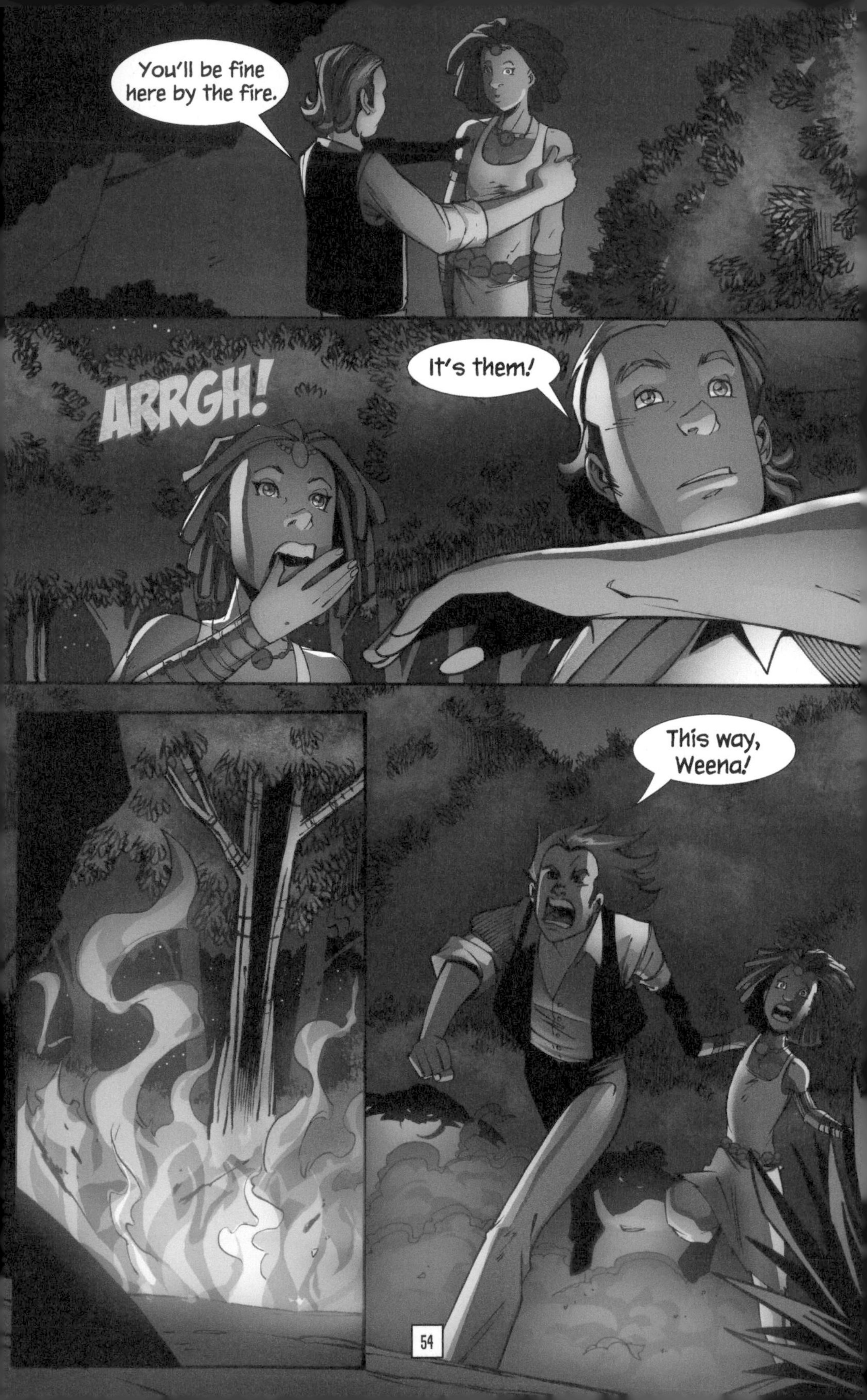
You'll be fine here by the fire.
ARRGH!
It's them!
This way, Weena!

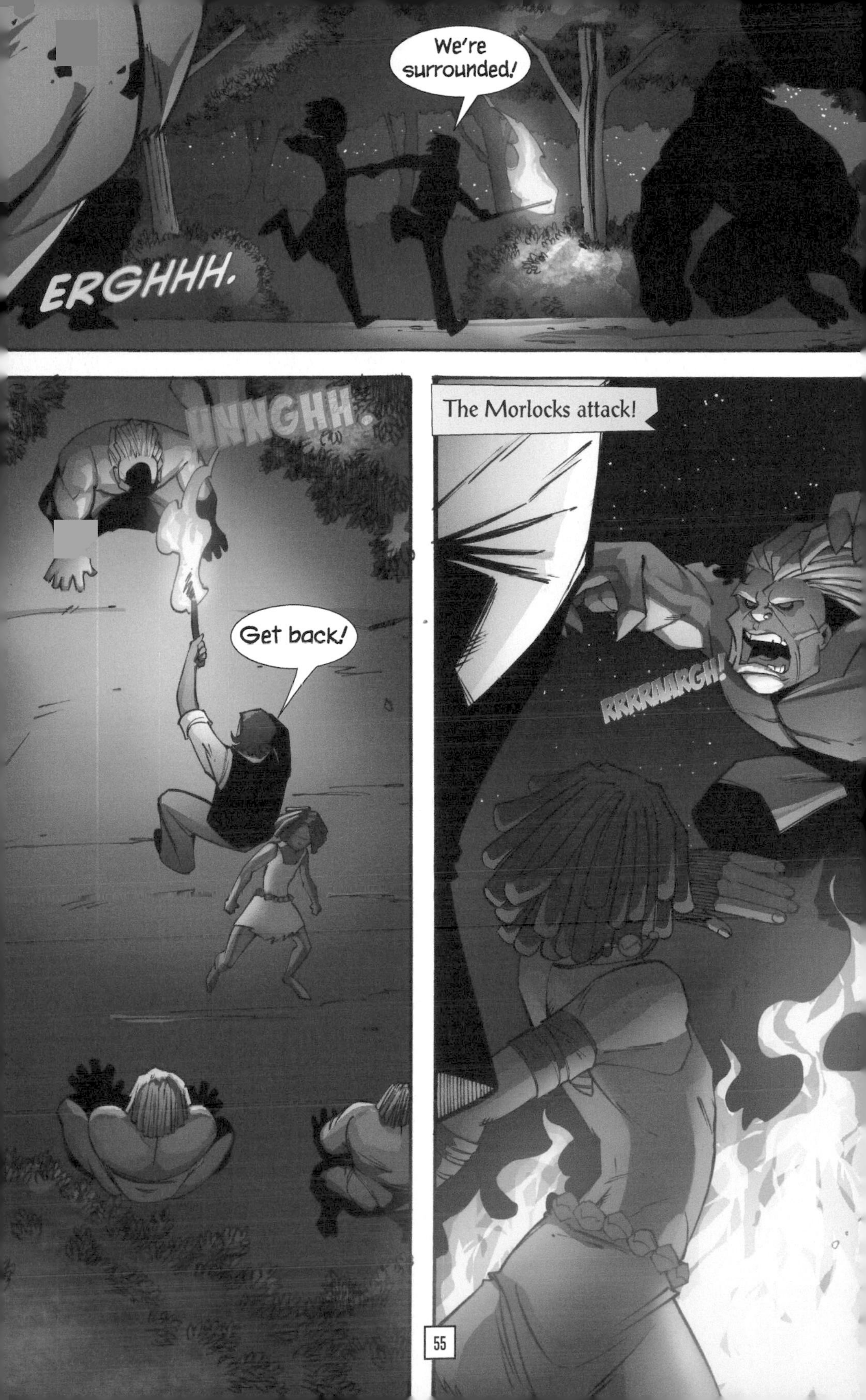
We're surrounded!
ERGHHH.
UNNGHH.
Get back!
The Morlocks attack!
RRRRAARGH!

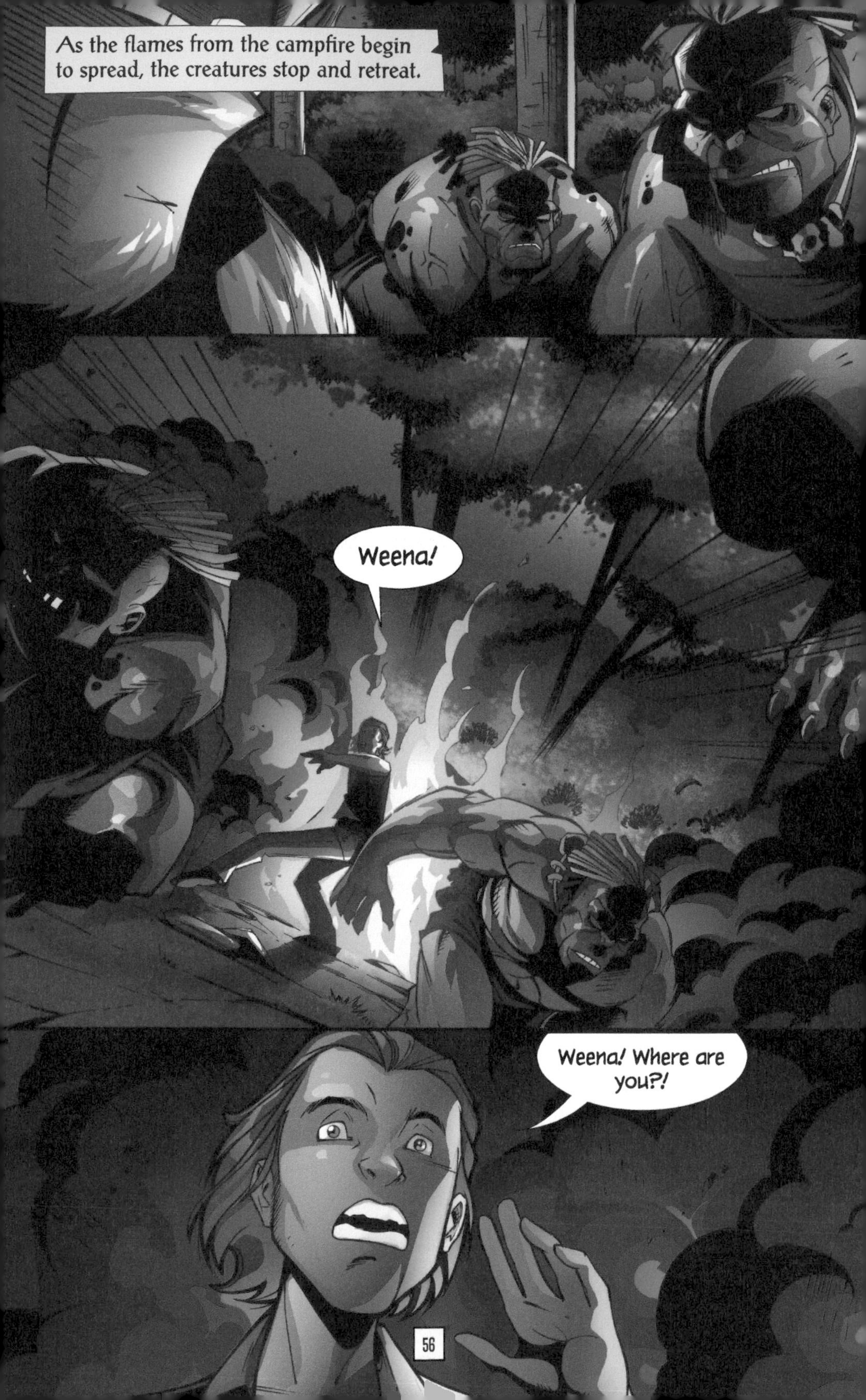
As the flames from the campfire begin to spread, the creatures stop and retreat.
Weena!
Weena! Where are you?!

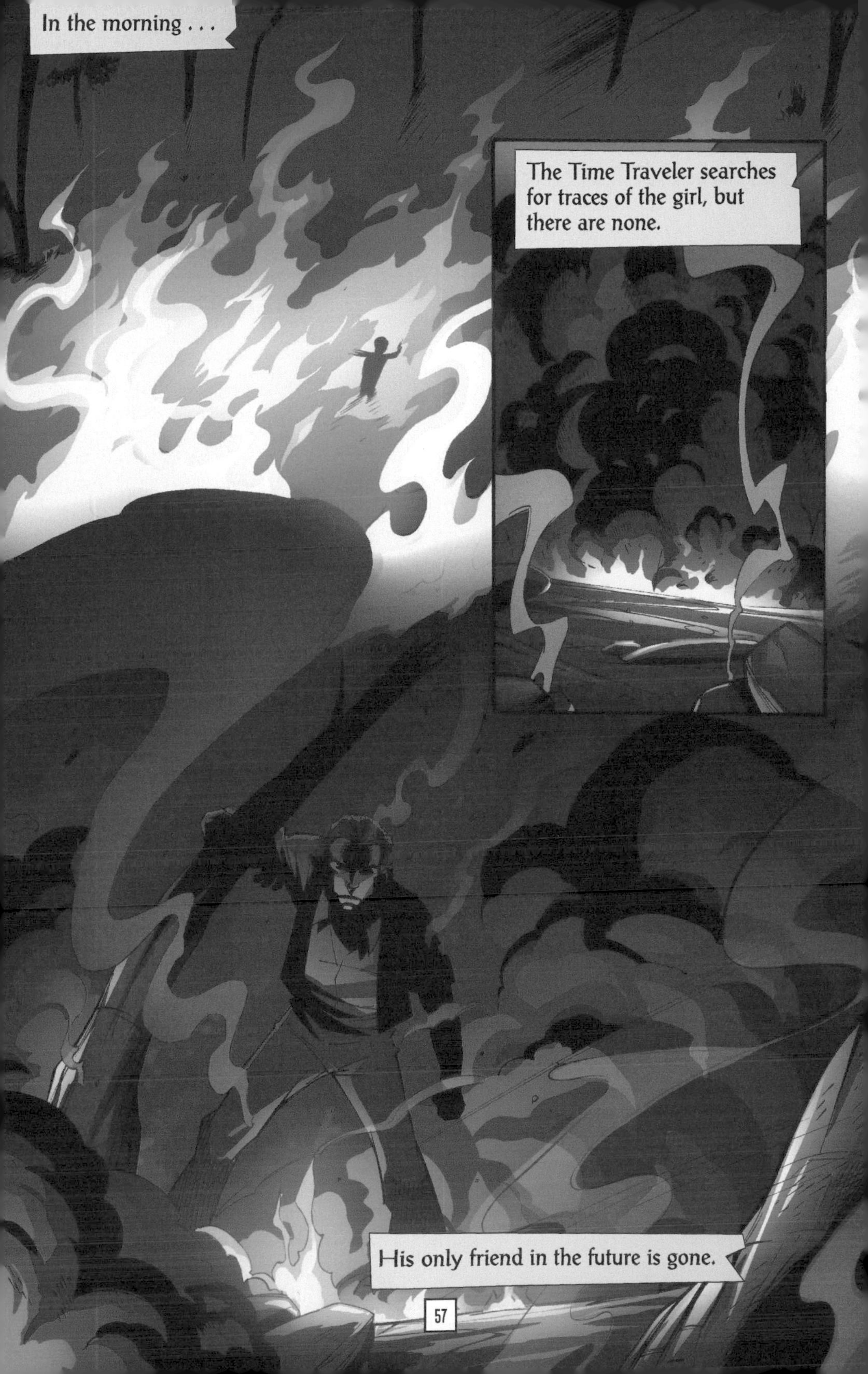
In the morning . . .
The Time Traveler searches for traces of the girl, but there are none.
His only friend in the future is gone.

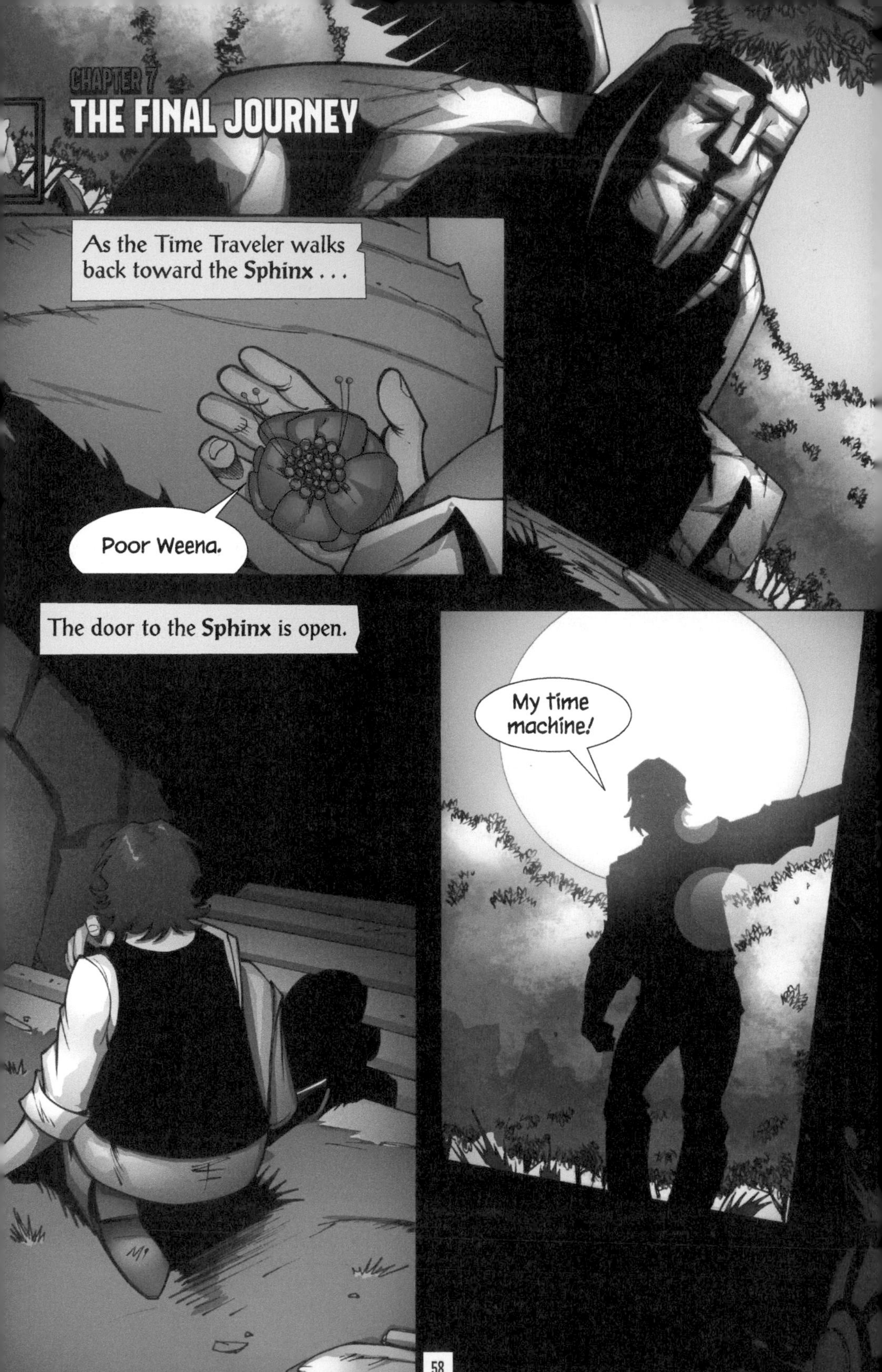
CHAPTER 7
THE FINAL JOURNEY
As the Time Traveler walks back toward the Sphinx . . .
Poor Weena.
The door to the Sphinx is open.
My time machine!

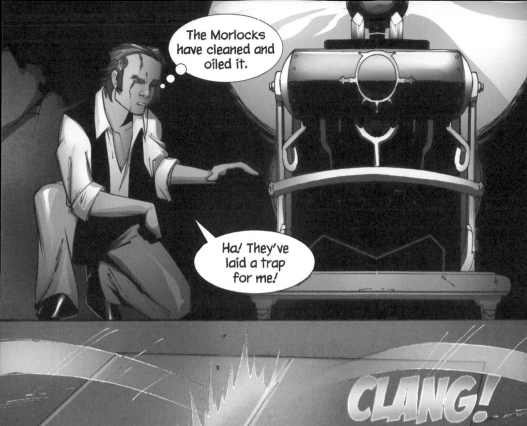

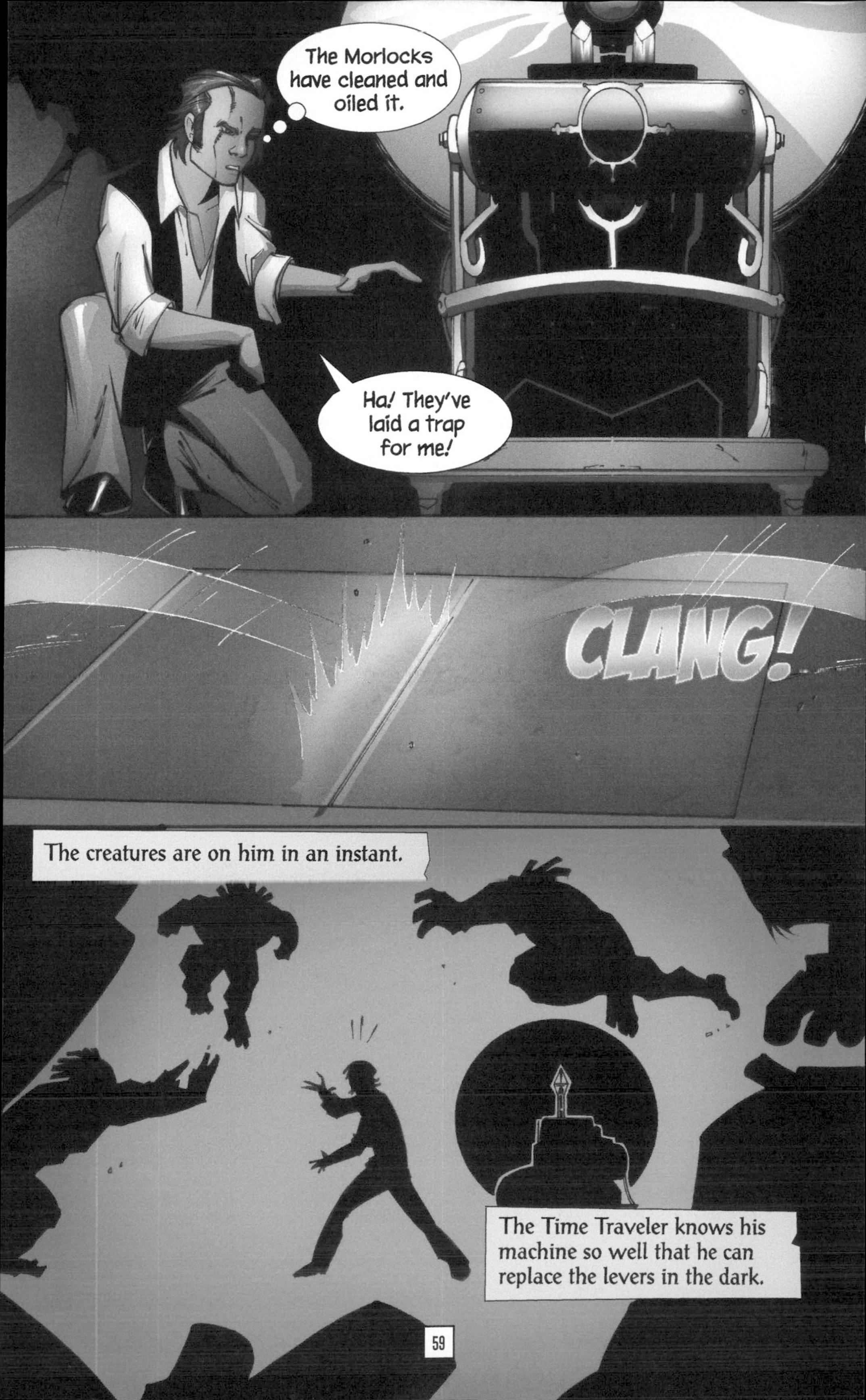
The Morlocks have cleaned and oiled it.
Ha! They've laid a trap for me!
CLANG!
The creatures are on him in an instant.
The Time Traveler knows his machine so well that he can replace the levers in the dark.

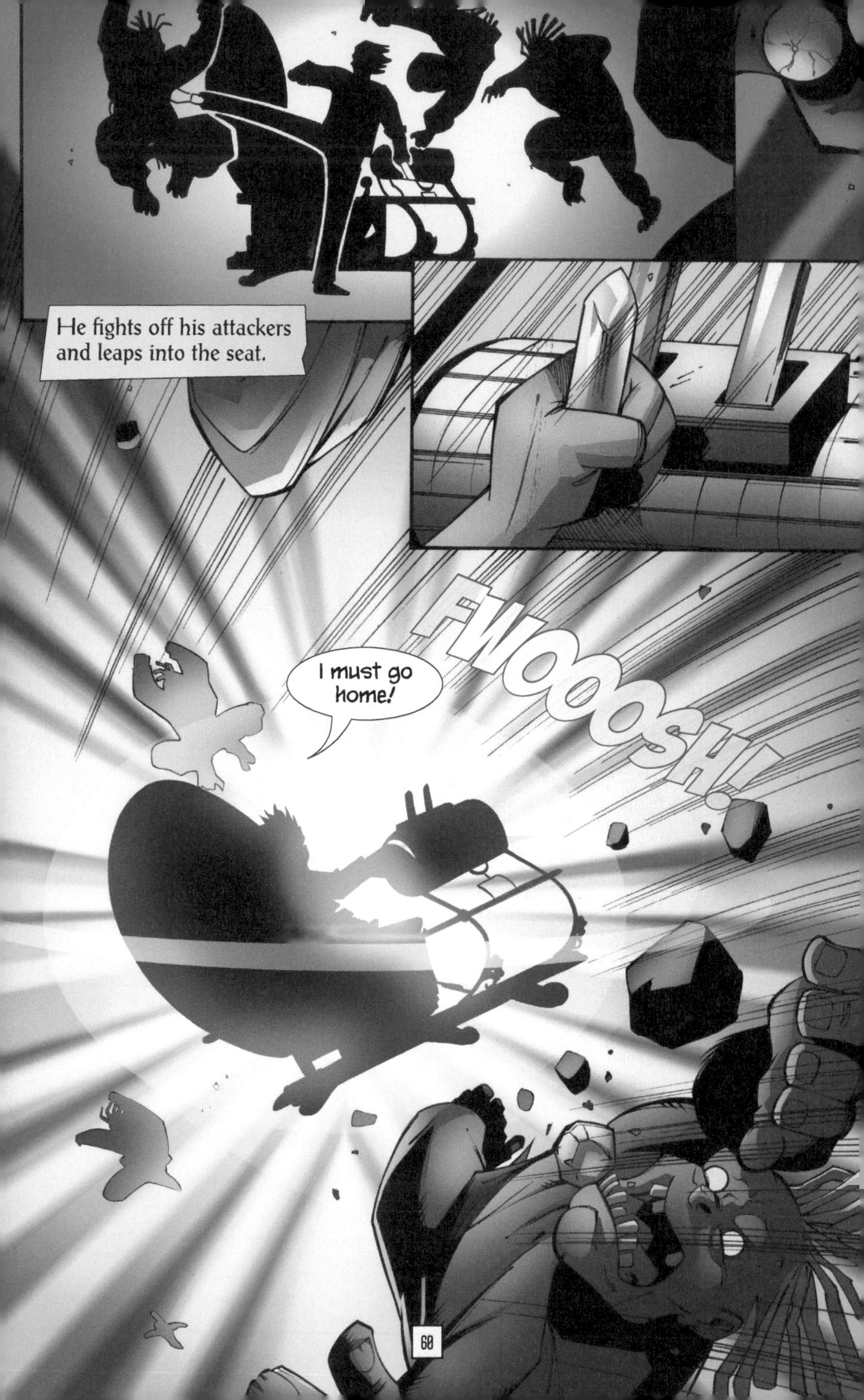
He fights off his attackers and leaps into the seat.
FWOOOSH!
I must go home!

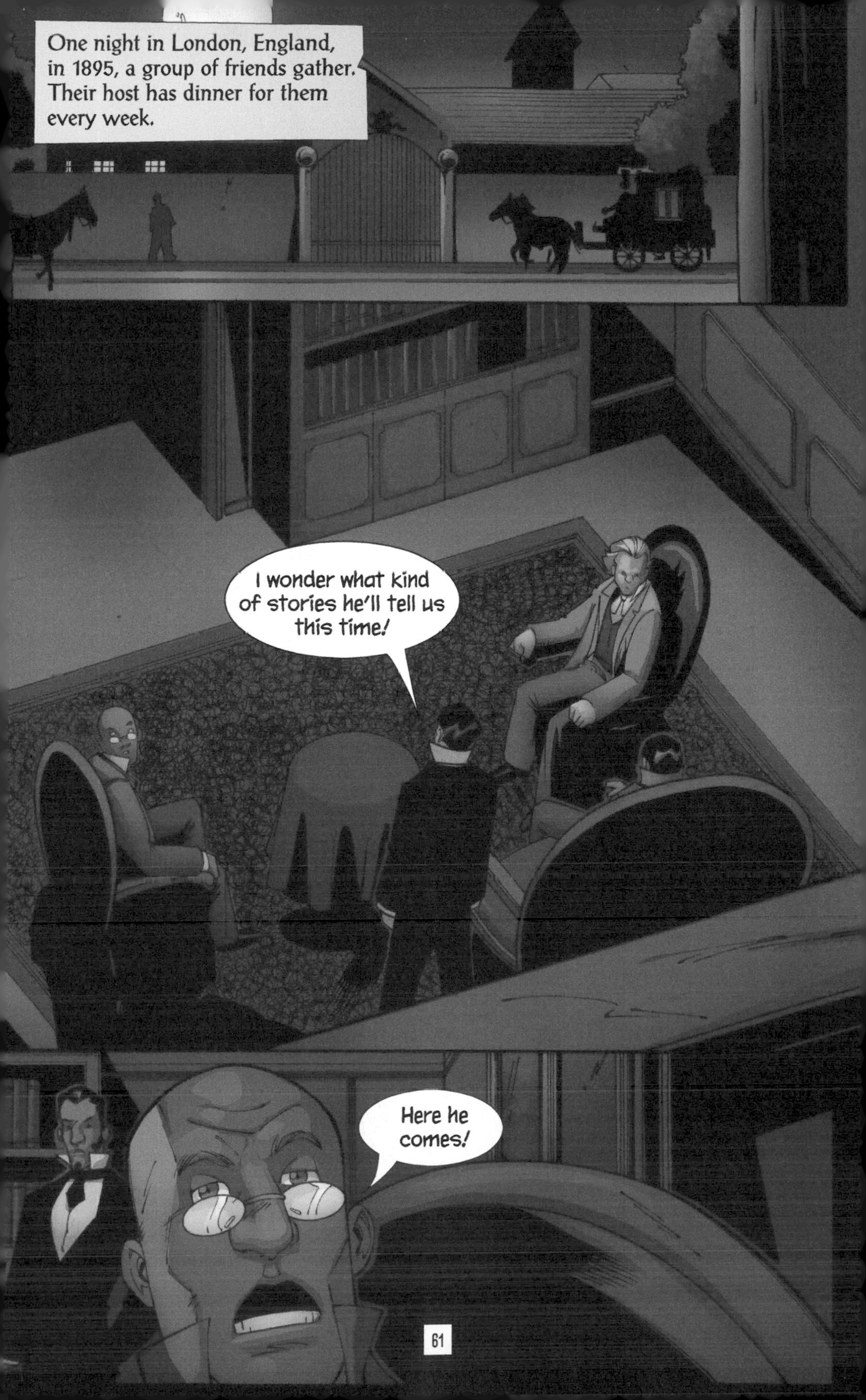
One night in London, England, in 1895, a group of friends gather. Their host has dinner for them every week.
I wonder what kind of stories he'll tell us this time!
Here he comes!

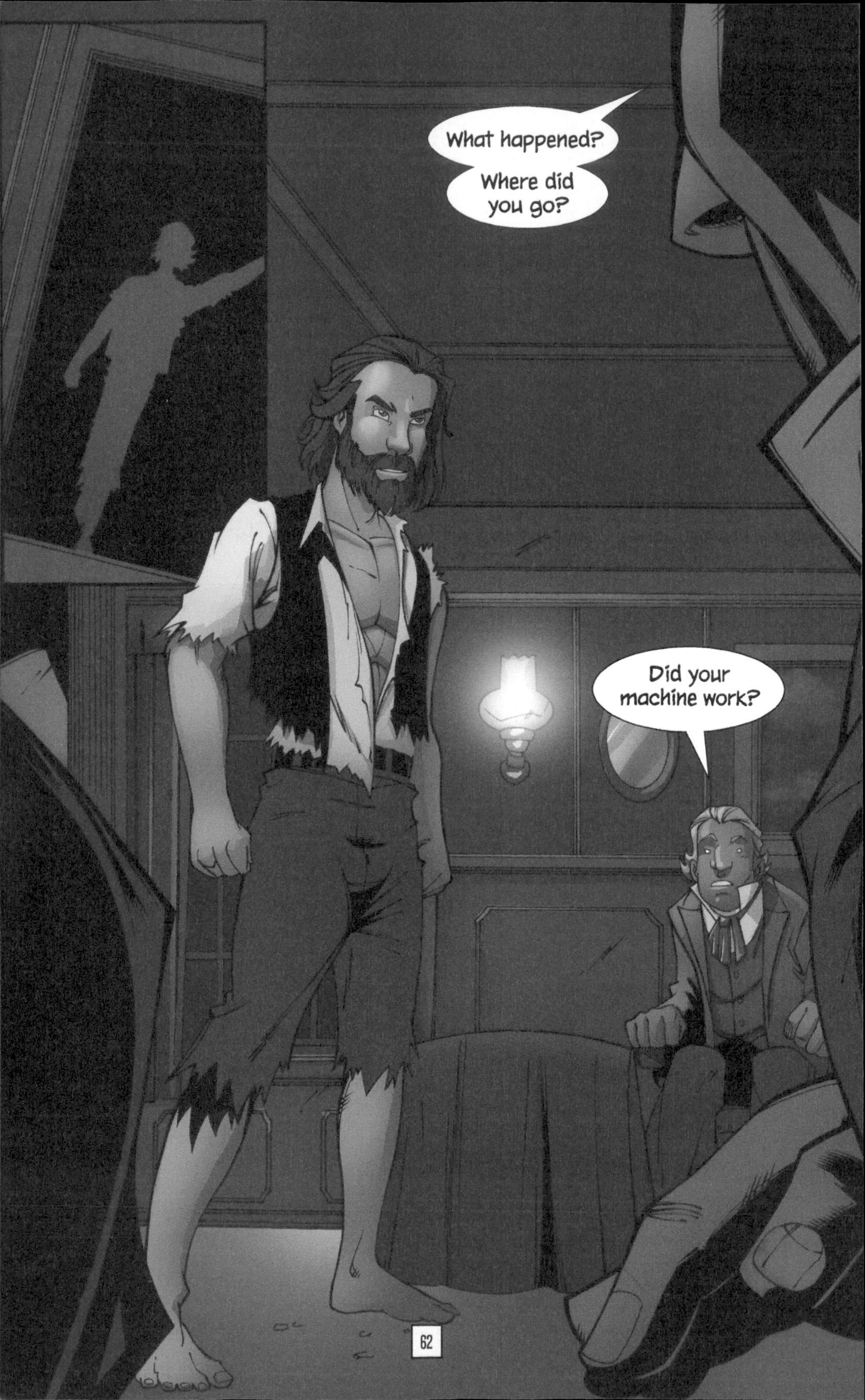
What happened?
Where did you go?
Did your machine work?

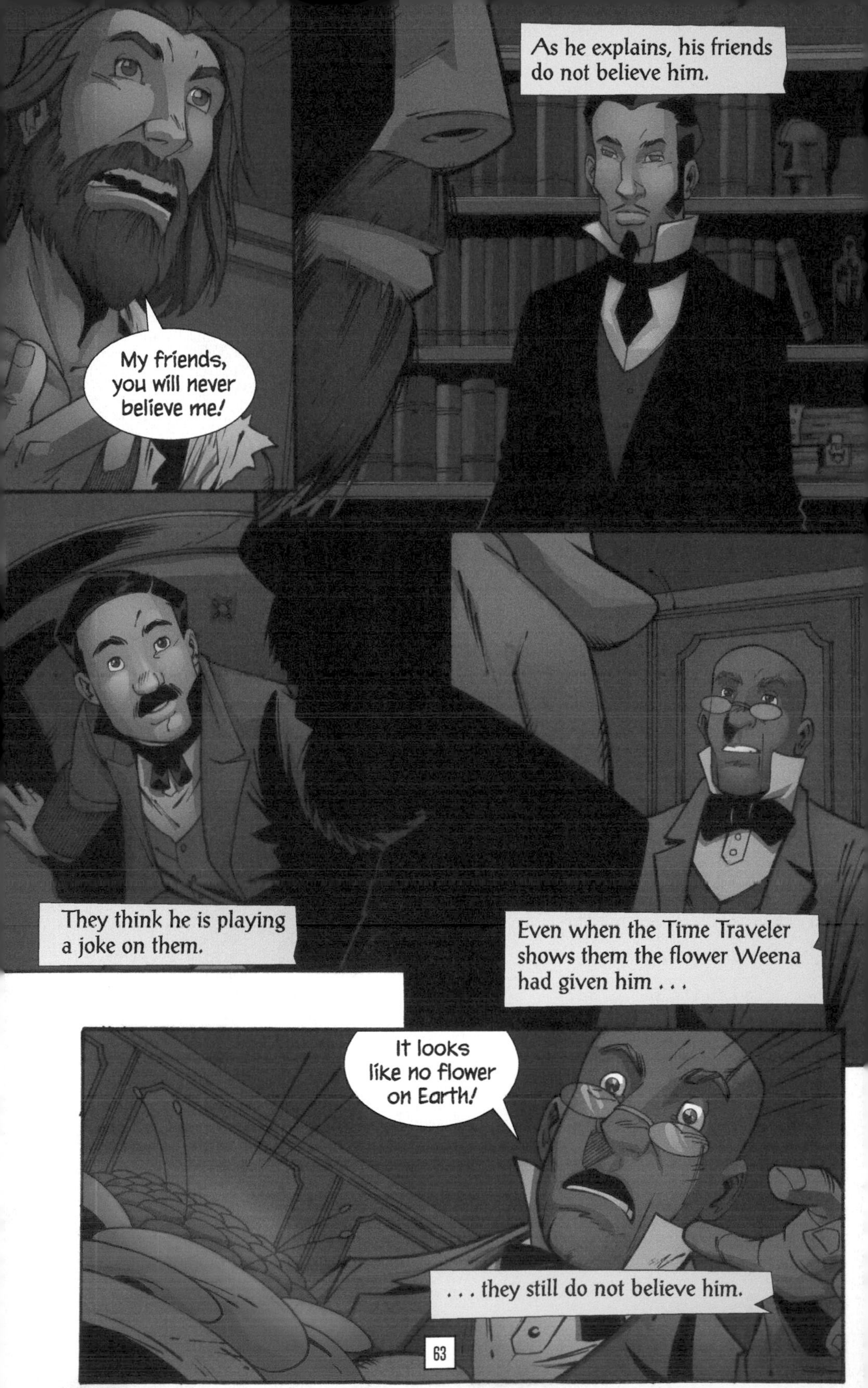
As he explains, his friends do not believe him.
My friends, you will never believe me!
They think he is playing a joke on them.
Even when the Time Traveler shows them the flower Weena had given him . . .
It looks like no flower on Earth!
. . . they still do not believe him.

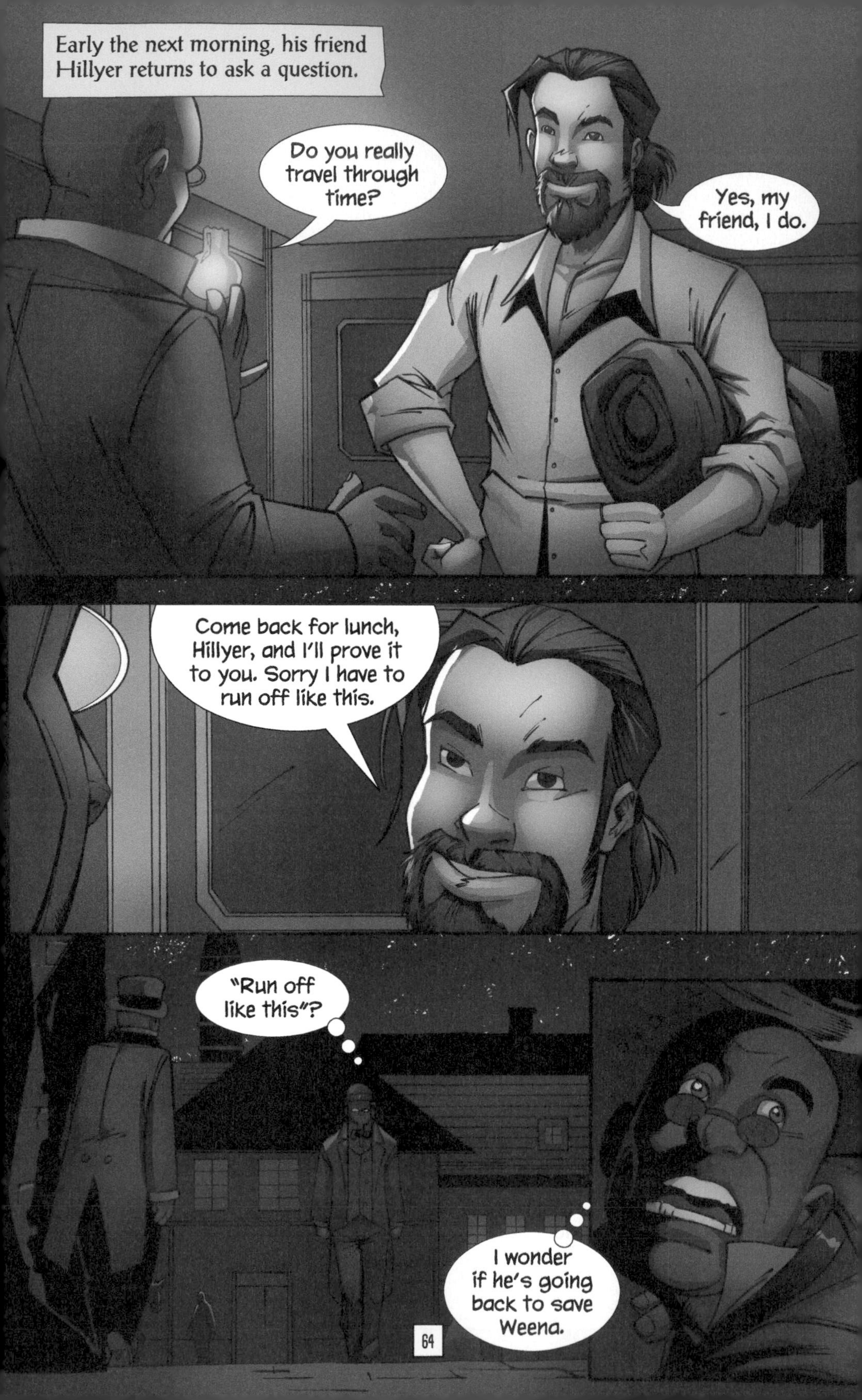
Early the next morning, his friend Hillyer returns to ask a question.
Do you really travel through time?
Yes, my friend, I do.
Come back for lunch, Hillyer, and I'll prove it to you. Sorry I have to run off like this.
"Run off like this"?
I wonder if he's going back to save Weena.

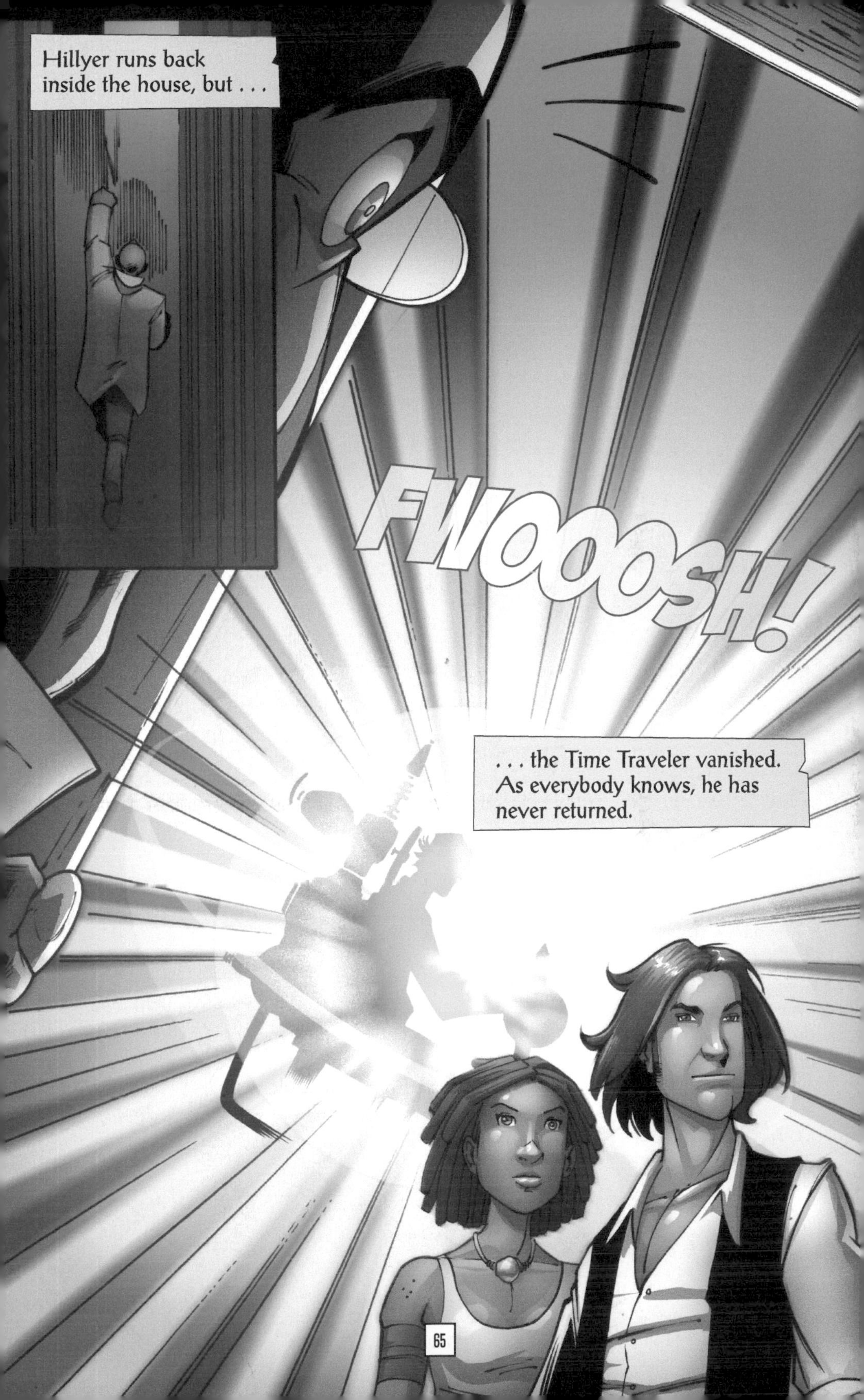
Hillyer runs back inside the house, but . . .
FWOOOSH!
. . . the Time Traveler vanished. As everybody knows, he has never returned.

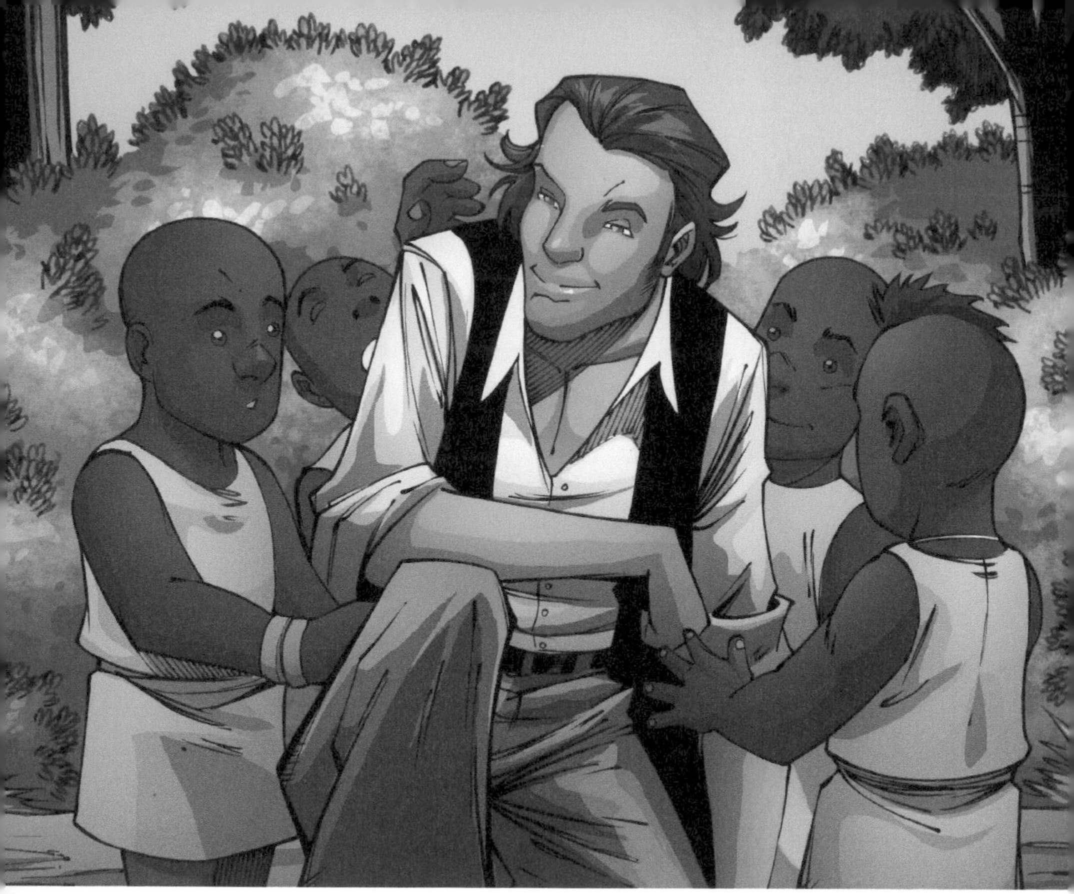

ABOUT THE RETELLING AUTHOR AND ILLUSTRATOR

Terry Davis is a father, a writer, and — in his words — "a fat old wrestling coach." He also teaches narrative and screenwriting at Minnesota State University, Mankato.

José Alfonso Ocampo Ruiz was born in 1975 in Macuspana, Tabasco in Mexico, where the temperature is just as hot as the sauce is. He became a comic book illustrator when he was 17 years old and has worked on many graphic novels since then. Alfonso has illustrated several graphic novels, including retellings of *Dracula* and *Pinocchio*.

GLOSSARY

descend (di-SEND)—to climb down or go to a lower level

gauges (GAYG-ehz)—instruments used for measuring things such as time, pressure, or distance

glade (GLAYD)—an open, grassy space surrounded by woods

horseless carriage (HORSS-lehss KAIR-ij)—another name for an automobile; people called the first automobiles horseless carriages because they moved without being pulled by a horse

livestock (LYV-stok)—animals raised on a farm, usually for food or to help with work; cows, sheep, and horses are all livestock.

Queen Victoria (KWEEN vik-TOR-ree-uh)—ruler of the British Empire from 1837 to 1901

Sphinx (SFINGKS)—a female monster in Greek mythology that has a woman's head, a lion's body, and wings

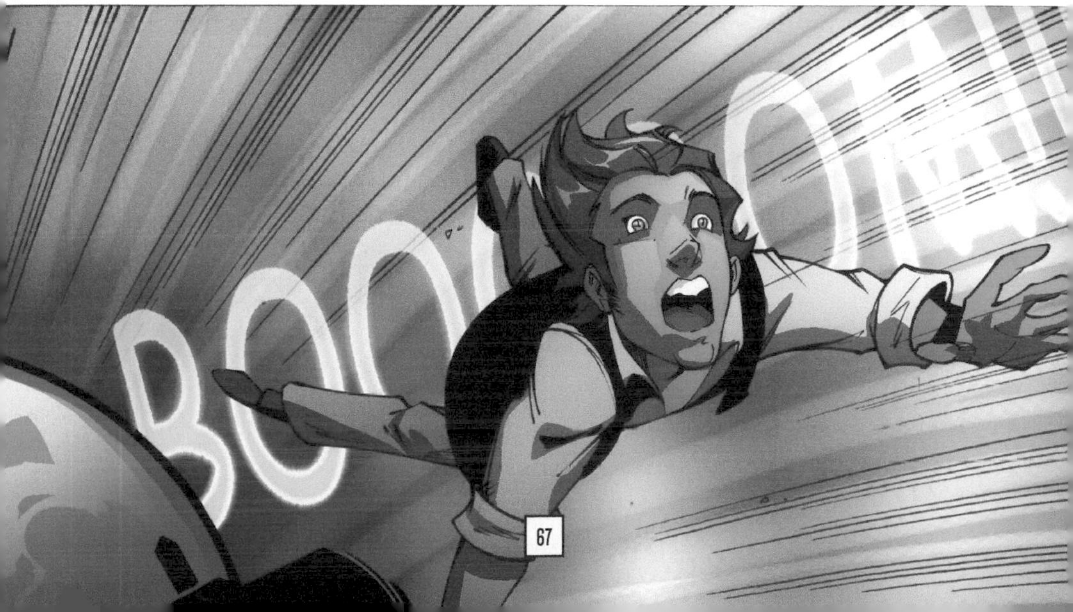
BOOOOM!

COMMON CORE ALIGNED
READING QUESTIONS

1. Think about the different ways that the Eloi, the Weena, and the Morlocks live. Compare and contrast their different ways of life, citing similarities and differences you've found within the art and text in this book. *("Compare and contrast the point of view from which different stories are narrated.")*

2. H.G. Wells is often considered to be one of the forebears of modern science fiction. What happens in the story to make it qualify as science fiction? *("Refer to details and examples in a text when explaining what the text says explicitly and when drawing inferences from the text.")*

3. At the beginning of the story, the Time Traveler is ridiculed by his friends about his model time machine. What does the teasing make the Time Traveler do? Afterward, how does he feel about his decisions, and how do you know? *("Describe in depth a character . . . drawing on specific details in the text.")*

4. "Time" is a significant theme in this story. Where in time does the Time Traveler go? Why? If you had a time machine, would you go into the past or into the future? What date would you like to visit? *("Determine a theme of a story.")*

5. How do the illustrations in this book work together with the words to bring the story alive? Does it make you want to read the original book that does not have pictures? Why or why not? *("Explain major differences between . . . structural elements.")*

COMMON CORE ALIGNED
WRITING QUESTIONS

1. Write a short, creative story in which you are the Time Traveler's assistant when you both travel to 802,171 CE. Would you enjoy the experience? Why or why not? *("Orient the reader by establishing a situation and introducing a narrator.")*

2. Do you think it is wise to travel in time to the past? What about the future? Why? What in this story helps you come to your decisions? *("Write opinion pieces on topics or texts, supporting a point of view with reasons and information.")*

3. Make a list of all the significant events in *The Time Machine.* When you are done, write a short explanation why each event is important. *("Draw evidence from literary . . . texts to support analysis.")*

4. This story does not identify the real name of the Time Traveler. If you could pick a first and last name for him, what would you choose, why? Identify 2-3 specific character details that helped you choose his name. *("Describe in depth a character . . . drawing on specific details in the text.")*

5. Make a poster that illustrates the time period of 802,171 CE. as it is presented in this book. What words and illustrations would you use on your poster to get people interested in traveling to that time period? *("Produce clear and coherent writing in which the development and organization are appropriate to task, purpose, and audience.")*

READ THEM ALL!

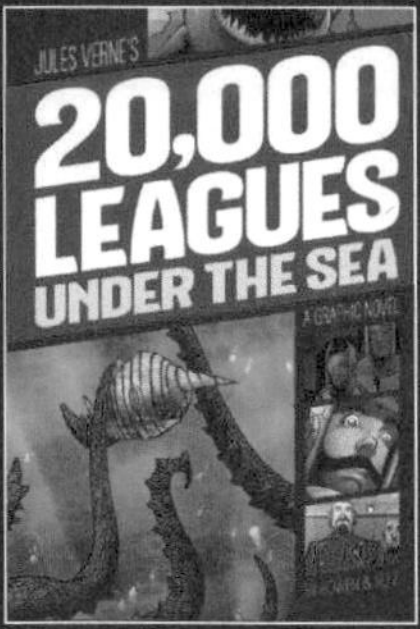
JULES VERNE'S
20,000 LEAGUES UNDER THE SEA
A GRAPHIC NOVEL

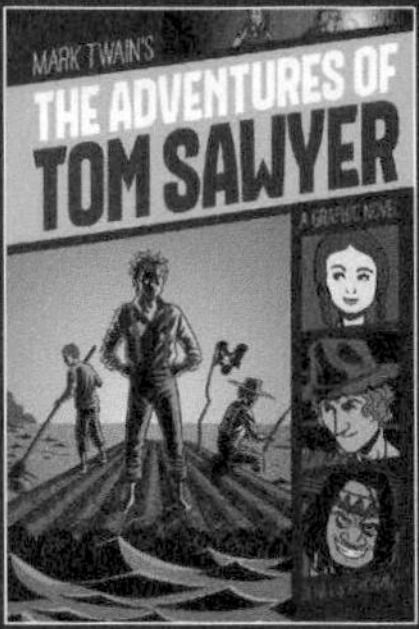
MARK TWAIN'S
THE ADVENTURES OF TOM SAWYER
A GRAPHIC NOVEL

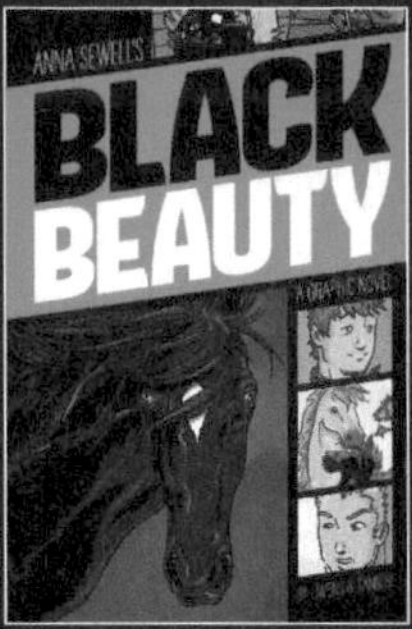
ANNA SEWELL'S
BLACK BEAUTY
A GRAPHIC NOVEL

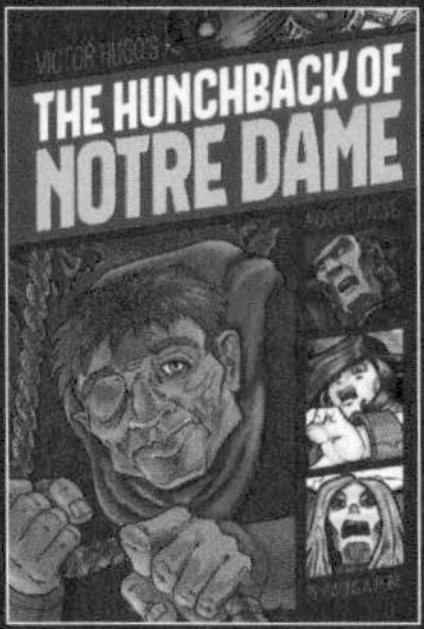
VICTOR HUGO'S
THE HUNCHBACK OF NOTRE DAME

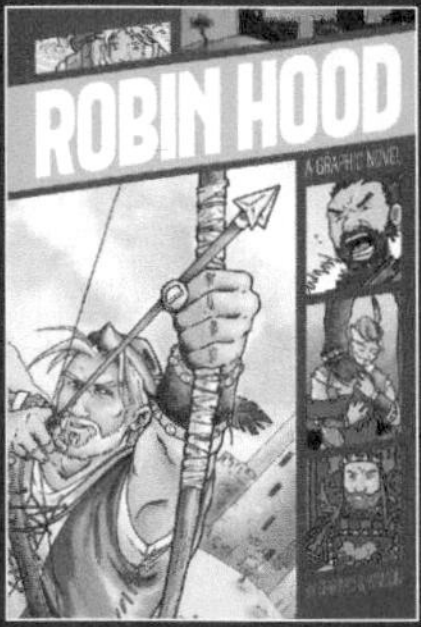
ROBIN HOOD
A GRAPHIC NOVEL

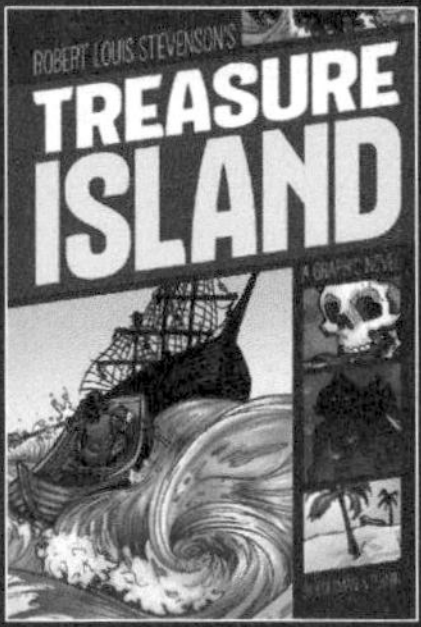
ROBERT LOUIS STEVENSON'S
TREASURE ISLAND
A GRAPHIC NOVEL

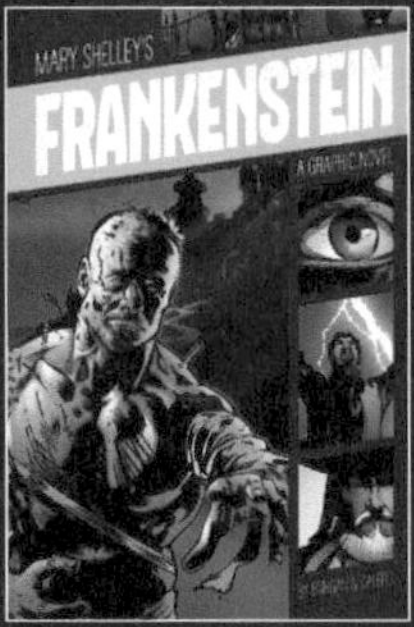
MARY SHELLEY'S
FRANKENSTEIN
A GRAPHIC NOVEL

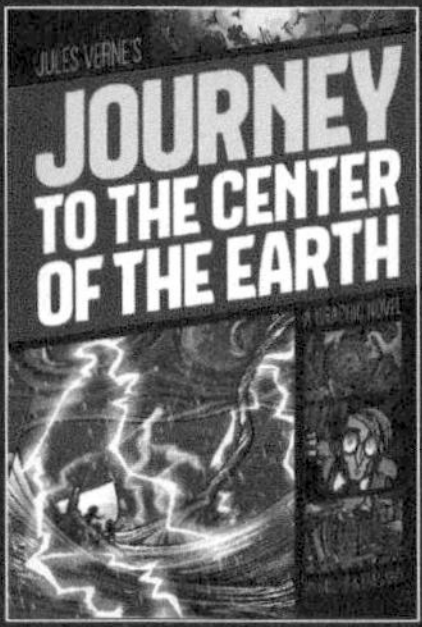
JULES VERNE'S
JOURNEY TO THE CENTER OF THE EARTH
A GRAPHIC NOVEL

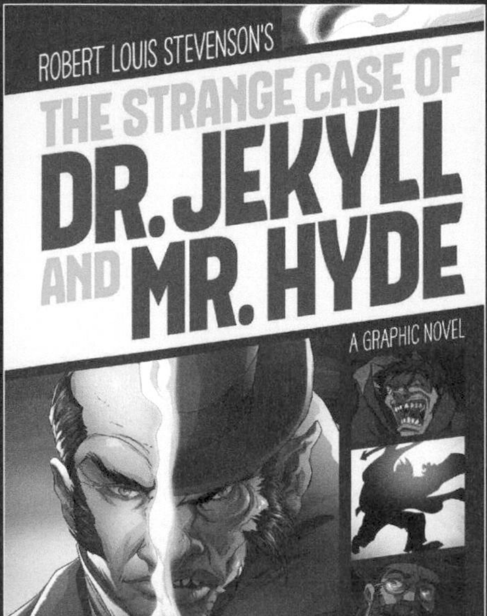
ROBERT LOUIS STEVENSON'S
THE STRANGE CASE OF DR. JEKYLL AND MR. HYDE
A GRAPHIC NOVEL
BY BOWEN & FERRAN

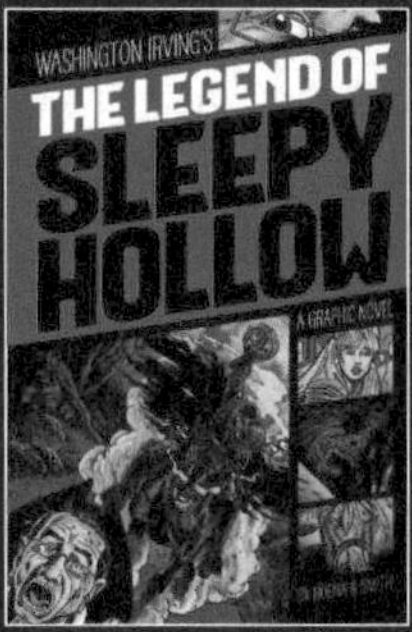
WASHINGTON IRVING'S
THE LEGEND OF SLEEPY HOLLOW
A GRAPHIC NOVEL

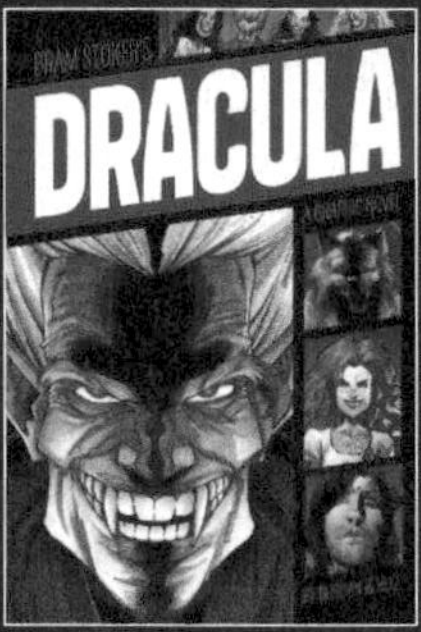
BRAM STOKER'S
DRACULA

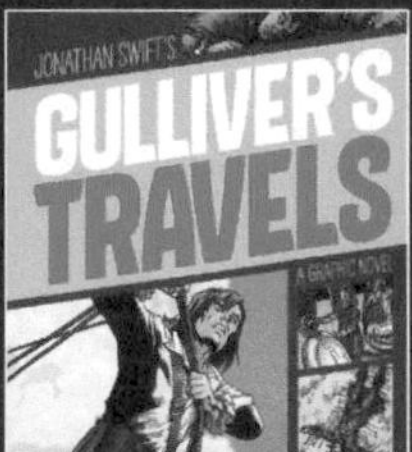
JONATHAN SWIFT'S
GULLIVER'S TRAVELS
A GRAPHIC NOVEL

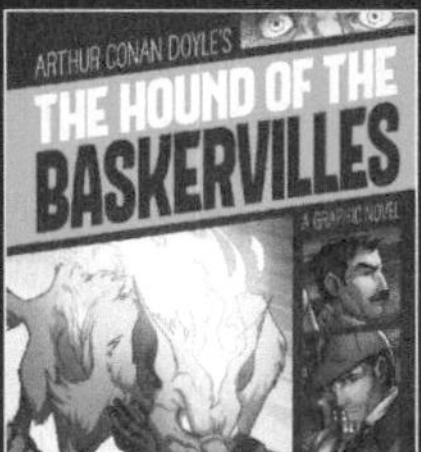
ARTHUR CONAN DOYLE'S
THE HOUND OF THE BASKERVILLES
A GRAPHIC NOVEL

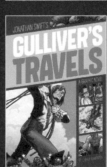

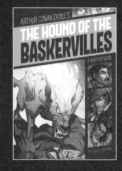

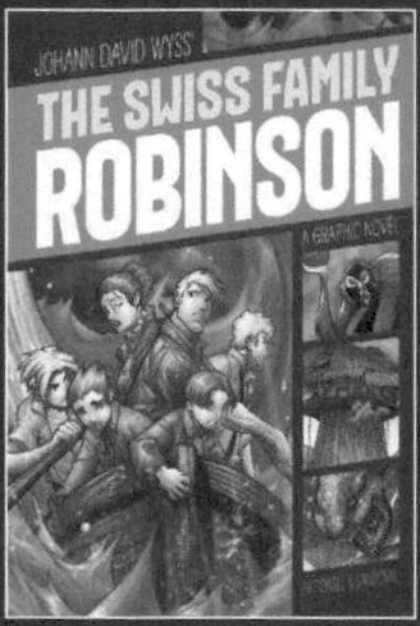
JOHANN DAVID WYSS'
THE SWISS FAMILY ROBINSON
A GRAPHIC NOVEL

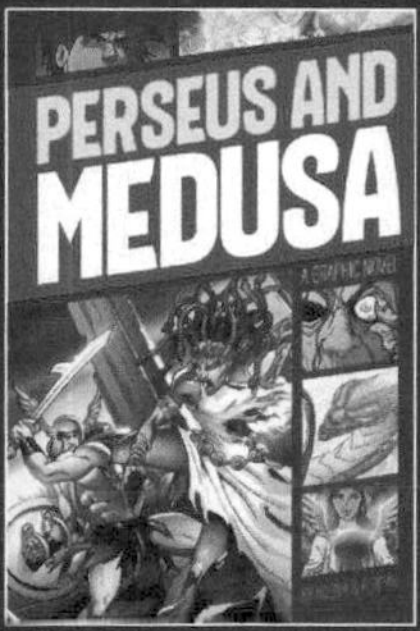
PERSEUS AND MEDUSA
A GRAPHIC NOVEL

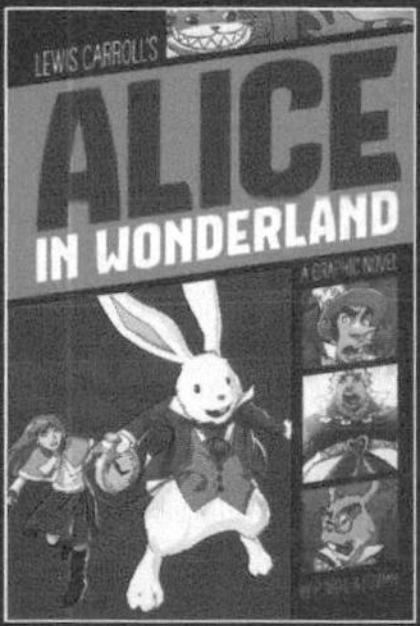
LEWIS CARROLL'S
ALICE IN WONDERLAND
A GRAPHIC NOVEL

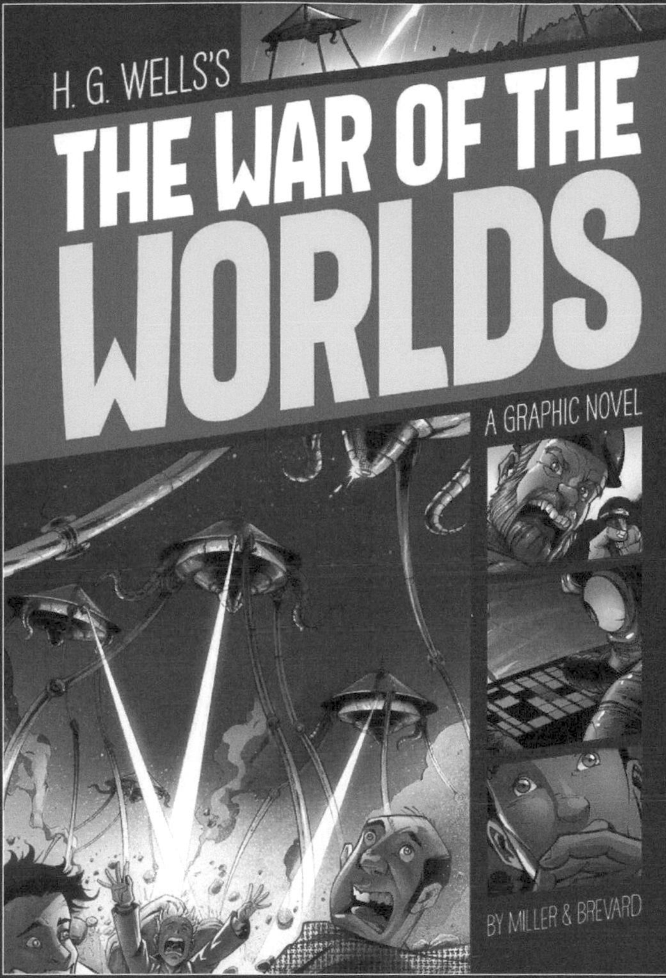
H. G. WELLS'S
THE WAR OF THE WORLDS
A GRAPHIC NOVEL
BY MILLER & BREVARD

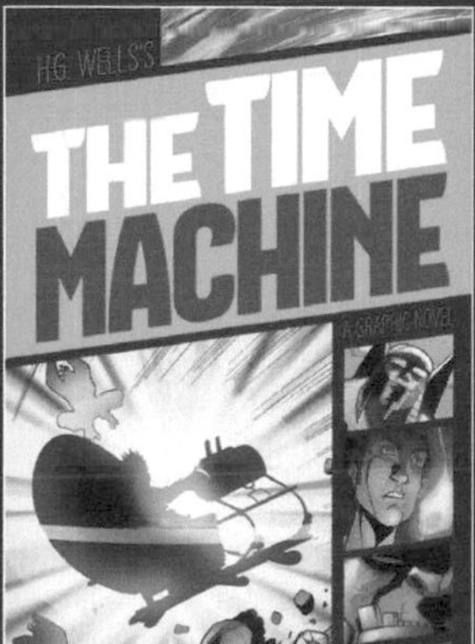
H.G. WELLS'S
THE TIME MACHINE
A GRAPHIC NOVEL
BY DAVIS & RUIZ

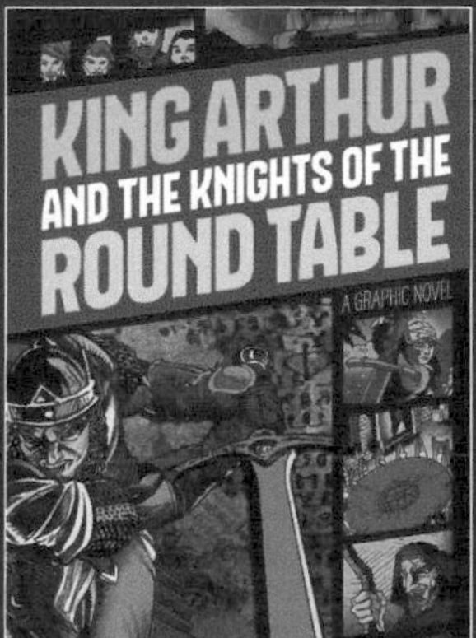
KING ARTHUR AND THE KNIGHTS OF THE ROUND TABLE
A GRAPHIC NOVEL

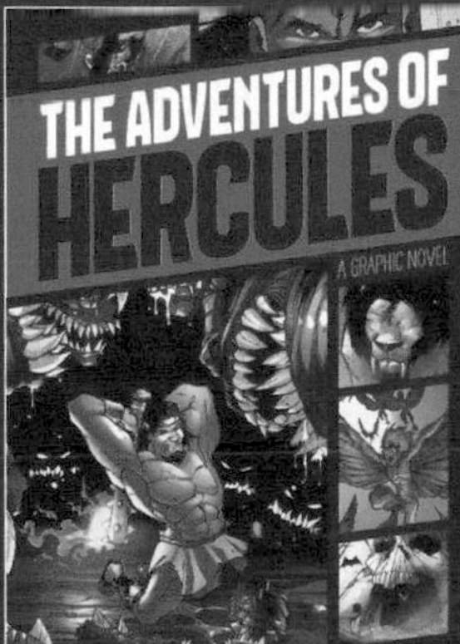
THE ADVENTURES OF HERCULES
A GRAPHIC NOVEL
BY POWELL & RUIZ